Hawley Smart

Tie and Trick

Vol. 3

Hawley Smart

Tie and Trick
Vol. 3

ISBN/EAN: 9783337376086

Printed in Europe, USA, Canada, Australia, Japan

Cover: Foto ©Andreas Hilbeck / pixelio.de

More available books at **www.hansebooks.com**

TIE AND TRICK

A Melodramatic Story.

BY

HAWLEY SMART.

AUTHOR OF " BREEZIE LANGTON," "THE GREAT TONTINE," "AT FAULT,"
" FROM POST TO FINISH," ETC., ETC.

IN THREE VOLUMES.

VOL. III.

LONDON—CHAPMAN AND HALL
LIMITED.
1885.

WESTMINSTER:
PRINTED BY NICHOLS AND SONS,
25, PARLIAMENT STREET.

CONTENTS.

VOLUME III.

TIE AND TRICK.

CHAPTER I.

THE UNDERGROUND MAIL.

LEROUX had attained his object; he had opened communication with the captives. That very afternoon he had found out Chisel and dictated that note. It could not be too simple, he thought; a note that if it fell into wrong hands should commit nobody. It would be well to feel his way cautiously before anything compromising passed between him and the brigands. But in all his experiences of the criminal classes he had rarely found much difficulty in persuading them to sell their comrades for gold. It required tact, doubtless; the bribe must be dangled before their eyes delicately in the first place. There is little harm, for instance, in smuggling a letter—more especially when you are well paid for doing so. Leroux read the contents of this note over to Giovanni next day, and then gave it to him unfastened.

"You can show it to anybody," he remarked; "and, if you think it can possibly work any harm to Count Patroceni or his men, do not deliver it. It is only natural that the friends of the prisoners here in Naples should want to let them know that every effort is being made for their release."

Giovanni said nothing for some few minutes, but his eyes sparkled at the sight of the gold and the basket of wine which Leroux handed him.

"There can't be any harm in that bit of a note," he said at length. "I'll look it over again; but I think I can promise to get that forwarded for you."

The police-agent suppressed the smile that rose to his lips; it was as he had suspected; it was evident to him by Giovanni's manner that he could not read. He put the note away carefully in his pocket without looking at it. What was to prevent his examining it then and there? Simply his inability to understand it. Leroux had taken all this into his calculation. Now the question was—Had Giovanni any friend in Naples to whom he could venture to show it? The police-agent thought not. It was clear that Giovanni looked upon it that there was great risk in interfering with the brigands. It was probable that he would not wish any one to know that he held communication with them. Again Leroux was right; this was just his companion's dilemma. He could not read that note himself, nor, save Matteo, did he know any one in Naples that he could trust to tell him its contents. He was not very likely to make a confidant of Matteo in the present state of his feelings with regard to that worthy. All this Leroux had counted on before making his proposition. He guessed that the greater part of the brigands were ignorant peasants, neither able to read nor write. It would not do to risk it the first time, but let one or two harmless notes pass, and they would no longer care whether the communication was open or closed. In a few days Leroux thought there was every probability of obtaining the intelligence he wanted, namely, what were their numbers, what were their habits, what hour would be most suitable for surprising the camp, and, above all, how far did their scouts extend? He meant to be very cautious; but if ever there was a case in which Talleyrand's famous maxim required to be rigidly adhered to on the part of a police-agent it was now. "Above all, *point de zèle!*" To rescue Sir Jasper

and his party and at the same time to
capture his abductors was an operation so
delicate and involving such risk that most
men, in Leroux's place, would have hesitated
to attempt it. Let a life be sacrificed and
there would be much outcry on the part
of the English Government. Leroux quite
understood what that meant. When a
strong nation begins to bully a weaker one
the latter casts eagerly about for a scapegoat. There was no doubt in Leroux's
mind as to who would be the scapegoat
in this case. Let him fail, and he would
be held as responsible for any loss of life
that might occur as Patroceni himself. But
Leroux was of the stuff of which heroes are
made, with nerves of iron and an ambition
insatiable, two qualities which have gone
far to make great generals or great rulers
for the most part. The unsatisfied lust for
territory, main stimulus of your great
conquerors, from Alexander to Napoleon.
Anyhow, Leroux had got his game in his

own hands, for those with power to interfere in it were in complete ignorance of his manœuvres.

Hammerton all this while was strenuously endeavouring to bring matters to a conclusion, but the hurrying of the raising of money is a weary task, as many a bold bettor or reckless spendthrift has found to his cost. The anxiety to lend, even at the most exorbitant interest, is utterly incommensurate with the desire to borrow; and, though Hammerton, fretful and fidgety, did his best to hurry Messrs. Toldi and Kratz, yet these accommodating bankers declared such a sum as he wanted could not be collected under two or three weeks. He was honestly desirous of doing his best, but Hammerton had far too much experience not to know that, however unimpeachable your securities, thousands are not plucked like fruit in an orchard. In a small way he had seen plenty of this sort of thing in his time; and, chafe though he might at the

delay, he was honestly convinced that the
bankers were doing their best. It may be
doubted whether time did not hang heavier
on his hands than on those of the captives
in the woods above Amalfi. There is not
very much to do in Naples, and Hammerton
thought it judicious to expose himself as
little as might be. What was to be the
outcome of all this, as far as he was concerned, even when brought to a satisfactory
conclusion ? Maude was irretrievably lost
to him, while he himself would stand de-
nounced as a card-sharper before every club
in London. True his denouncers might not
be able quite to establish their case, but
their asseverations would be quite strong
enough to throw a taint about him impossible to tide over. A man's honour in those
days—or nigh a score of years ago—was as
easily tarnished as a looking-glass. We
have changed all that and are changing it
still more day by day. We don't make quite
so much fuss about these trifles as of old,

and it is possible to do on the racecourse or
at the card-table things which would have
once put the perpetrators out of court.   It
was not at all that he was reformed.   There
are vices that consume a man, that once
they have seized him in their grip he is
helpless to struggle with, and none more so
than this.   Once the gambler has taken to
" assisting fortune " he is as little likely to
refrain as the opium-eater from the con-
sumption of his favourite drug.   Hammerton
to some extent recognised this ; he had lost
all his money, forfeited his chances, and im-
bibed a fatal passion for play.   " Why," he
thought, " should he not utilise his knowledge—why not practise those chicaneries
that, used against himself in his neophyte
days, had doubtless brought him to his
ruin ? "   Still, on the subject of rescuing his
uncle and his party, he was determined to
do his best, and had the slightest inkling of
M. Leroux's tortuous scheming fallen within
his ken he would have opposed it tooth and

nail—better judge of the gravity of the situation perhaps than the police-agent. The Captain had enjoyed the privilege of Patroceni's intimacy, and knew infinitely better than Leroux of what the Count was capable. And yet the archives of the bureau had told Leroux a good deal concerning his antagonist. But just as Hammerton would have sat down to confront the most *rusé écarté*-player in all Paris, so would the police-agent have backed himself to outwit the most accomplished *escroc* in all Europe.

Leroux's scheme was so far a success. He speedily found himself in constant communication with the brigands. The little *déjeuner* with Giovanni at that sleepy old tavern in the suburbs had become almost a daily institution. The bandit asked nothing better. He approved of the cookery, he approved of the wine, and in the matter of that the police-agent was ever liberal. Postage was paid for with a lavish hand, and, as far as thick-witted

Giovanni could see, the correspondence was perfectly harmless. Unluckily, that fact was precisely what was perplexing M. Leroux. His notes might be guarded, but they were nothing to the careful responses he received. They were all signed " Cyril Wheldrake "; but, as the police-agent said irritably to himself, " If ever there was a man who hesitated at doing something for freedom it is my correspondent. There is no getting the smallest bit of information out of him. What is the use of such a note as this ? "

" Thanks for yours. Glad to hear things are going on satisfactorily. Shall only be too delighted when all arrangements are complete ; thoughtful of you to write.

"CYRIL WHELDRAKE."

" Now," thought the police-agent, " it has been rather waste of both money and time to get into communication with a man who has not more nerve than this. He must understand what I mean. He surely can guess that his friends from the outside are curious to know how things are going on in the camp. A man with an ounce of common sense could comprehend all this without putting me to the risk of asking such a question on paper."

Wheldrake was no fool. He could understand all this. He gave Chisel great credit for having succeeded in establishing this correspondence between them, but then he very naturally supposed that he was in communication with his valet in Naples. Even had he known that it was the police who were prompting these epistles he would most decidedly have hesitated to furnish them with any information. The ransom might be stiff, but Wheldrake thoroughly comprehended that there was only one way out of the complication— namely, to pay the money. He knew well what he had risked by merely changing places with Hammerton. Glanfield and himself understood much more clearly than the others how near they had been to being shot off-hand. Sheer good-nature had a good deal to say to his sending even the very guarded replies that he did to Chisel's letters. M. Leroux was puzzled. It was all very well; with great difficulty and considerable expense he had set on foot an almost daily post between himself and the captives, but so far nothing could be more uninteresting than the correspondence. It might have been published in the journals, and Patroceni, his band, the whole country-side, and all the city left to make what they could of it, and the result would have been simply that Naples and Patroceni would know precisely what they did now. How was he to provoke this Signor Wheldrake into being more expansive in his communications? That was difficult. Leroux saw at once that his correspondent (though Chisel was the nominal writer) was a shrewd clear-headed man, who had no idea of compromising himself or his friends. Leroux quickly suspected, as was indeed the case, that Wheldrake would have infinitely have preferred that this correspondence had never been established. A terrible disappointment this to the police-agent. Time was everything, as he well knew, in this case; no information clearly to be got from Signor Wheldrake; and yet Leroux, thinking it over, came to the conclusion that neither his bribes of money or wine had been altogether thrown away. There was an increasing avidity on the part of Giovanni with regard to a surreptitious correspondence on which the postage ran to five gold pieces a letter. True, he had to share his spoil with his old comrade Pietro, but that worthy too was greedy of gold; and, although by no means the drunken swine that Giovanni was, like most of those men of the mountains he regarded wine and gambling as the two great luxuries of life. Two of the gold pieces, accompanied by a basket affording the wherewithal for a revel, had completely

won Pietro's adhesion to this unlicensed
post. He had submitted the notes to a
comrade, who, on the strength of having
been a courier, and picked up a slight command of English expletives, professed to
understand the language. He did to a very
limited extent, and was perfectly right
when, after laboriously spelling them out,
he pronounced Chisel's notes harmless, and
so M. Leroux had established a willing
agent at either end of the postal line he had
set up.

But, if he had got nothing out of the
correspondence, the police-agent had little
doubt that in a very short time the greed of
gold and the thirst for wine would put all
he wanted to know entirely at his disposal.
Like a Mephistopheles, whose business it is
to trade on the infirmities of our nature, and
armed with that great experience of criminal
humanity which his profession had taught
him, Leroux was assured that the two
deadliest baits to men of that type were

already in their mouths, only to be speedily
in their maws.   Pike-fishers give their
victims a measured time to gorge ; and M.
Leroux knew that he also must afford these
luckless pike of his hooking some short
grace to swallow the bait he so successfully
dangled before their eyes past all repudia-
tion.

———————————

CHAPTER II.

MATTEO SCENTS TREASON.

CAREFUL as Leroux had been to conceal his intimacy with Giovanni, he had aroused suspicion on the part of Matteo. The inn-keeper, as has been before said, was prone that way. The first thing that had attracted his attention was Giovanni's deviation from his usual habits. Unknown to that worthy he caught sight of him on the occasion when he had met Leroux in the Villa del Reale, previous to adjourning to that snug tavern, at which their meetings now habitually took place. That Giovanni should enter the gardens and not come for a glass of wine to the Pavilion was remarkable. The bandit had few acquaintances in the city, and even fewer haunts. During his brief visits to Naples, a room in the slums of La Vicaria to sleep in, and the tables outside the Pavilion at which to smoke and drink, were the two places between which Giovanni divided his time. Though Matteo had noticed him in the garden that morning, he had not seen him leave it in company with Leroux, and therefore his suspicions were not excited on that account. He thought that the bandit would shortly return to the mountains; but, wishing to learn something with regard to the negotiations for the release of the prisoners, he thought it worth while to make his way into La Vicaria one afternoon. He knew well where his comrades were in the habit of locating themselves on their visits to the city, and speedily ascertained that Giovanni had not yet returned to the camp.

This puzzled Matteo. He did not understand the man's lingering in Naples—it was
quite foreign to his usual habits ; on previous occasions Giovanni had usually been
accompanied by some of his comrades, and
not a day had passed but what he had
seen them in the Pavilion. Now the
bandit was apparently alone, and never
came near it. With what object had he
come into the town, what was he doing,
where did he spend his time, and above
all what wine-shop did he frequent? It
was a singular thing that it should never
occur to so shrewd a man as Matteo that
his old comrade might cherish feelings of
extreme rancour with regard to himself.
He never dreamt that the terrible punishment meted out by the Count was laid to
his door. So omnipotent was Patroceni in
Matteo's eyes that he would have deemed
it better to offend against all laws, human
and divine, sooner than fail in his fidelity
to the Count. That he should report every-

thing to his chief was to him a matter past question; that Patroceni should deal out punishment to them all was a thing no more to be disputed than the decrees of Providence: he had merely done his duty to his chief and his comrades; and if Giovanni had paid hardly for his offending what had he to do with it? He felt as a soldier might who had simply done his duty in reporting the fault of a comrade, and never dreamt that comrade cherished the most bitter resentment against him for having done so. It would have been perhaps better for Matteo had that idea struck him. Though shrewd and crafty he was not gifted with either physical strength or personal courage; and, supreme contempt as he had for Giovanni's wits, yet he had much too great a respect for his thews and sinews to run the risk of a personal collision. It was from no anxiety on his own account, but as a sheer matter of curiosity, that Matteo set himself the task of ascertaining how Giovanni passed his time in Naples. He did not suspect him of treachery, that is, a premeditated treachery; but being a man naturally suspicious, and withal aware of Giovanni's infirmity, he might well feel a little uneasy at the thought of his comrade hanging about the city. It was but the other day he had betrayed too much to a stranger in his drunkenness; who was to ensure his not doing so again? And, thanks to their late exploits, the brigands were in a more risky situation than they had been then. Their presence in the immediate vicinity of the city was then unsuspected, now it was notorious.

But, to his amazement, Matteo discovered that this was not quite so easy. It was not that he anticipated any real difficulty, but he had fancied that the people at Giovanni's lodgings would be able to tell him where that gentleman spent his days. But they could tell him nothing. As a rule, when

any of the band were in Naples, any of
those affiliated could find them without
difficulty. Now, the lodging-house keeper
could only say, "Surely, Signor Matteo,
you must know, for he takes his meals with
you as usual." I presume Matteo did not
think it necessary to confide to the good
lady that this was not the case; but he
marvelled a good deal where it was that his
old comrade did his eating and drinking.
That it would be easy to what our French
neighbours call "*filè*" Giovanni, Matteo
had no doubt; but, then, that required
time, and the innkeeper had his business to
attend to. Still it had to be done; and,
having ascertained from the good woman of
the house about what hour Giovanni was
accustomed to go out for his *déjeuner*,
Matteo made up his mind to dog his footsteps the next day.

In accordance with this resolution, nearly
an hour before the time at which Giovanni
was wont to issue from his lair, Matteo was

lounging in the street some little distance
off, but keeping a keen eye on the door.
No sooner did the bandit make his appearance than he followed him, and easily
tracked him to the old tavern to which
Leroux had introduced him. Having given
his old comrade time to settle himself,
Matteo made his way rather shyly to the
door of the half coffee-room, half-garden,
in which the *habitués* of the place were
wont to take their meals.

There is a freemasonry in all crafts, and
Matteo was an innkeeper. It is rather a
rule of the road with the better class of
this profession not only to take no money
but to entertain each other somewhat
liberally when one of the trade crosses their
threshold. Matteo certainly did not know
the host of the " Golden Bush "—it was a
retired house ; but it was very possible that
the landlord of the " Golden Bush " knew
him. The Pavilion was a tavern in the full
blaze of day, standing in the big public

gardens of Naples, and haunted by a very mixed *clientèle*. Visitors of all classes frequented the Villa del Reale, and sipped their coffee or drank their wine at the Pavilion.

Matteo saw that Giovanni had seated himself in a corner of the garden. A glance also showed him that he was known here; he would have liked to have stolen into the place, and watched Giovanni at his meal. But he was afraid of attracting the attention of the landlord. He by no means wished that Giovanni should see him; and, though he did not despair of evading his notice if left to himself, he was afraid that in a spirit of *camaraderie* the host of the "Golden Bush" might call attention to his presence. The man whom the king delights to honour is always the cynosure of all eyes, and in microscopic fashion the favoured guest of an hotel coffee-room always provokes much speculation amongst the other diners. He hesitated for a few minutes, and

then finally resolved not to risk it—he
would come there to-morrow, procure a
table in the back-ground, and await the
arrival of this renegade, who had deserted
his wine-flasks. He turned on his heel and
was going out when his attention was
arrested by a courteous salutation, and he
found himself bowing to the old gentleman
who had made his appearance in the Pavilion with Giovanni some few mornings
ago.

Leroux had recognised him at a glance,
and, though considerably put out at seeing
him, was much too shrewd to ignore his
presence. The two men passed with a bow,
and each asked himself, " What the deuce
had brought the other there?" Cunning
and suspicious, Matteo felt no doubt that
this old gentleman was there for the special
purpose of meeting Giovanni. Now, what
could be the meaning of that? Giovanni
was hardly an object upon whom the most
eccentric philanthropist would waste his

money or advice. Matteo knew from former experience that the sharers of Giovanni's revels were usually destined to pay the reckoning. "A pig, a hog, a dolt like that!" murmured the innkeeper. "What motive can that old man have in letting him swill wine at his expense? For, though I've not actually seen it, I could stake my life that Giovanni is waiting there for this stranger to fill his insatiable throttle. The thick-skulled sponge, no one would bathe him in wine except they hoped to get something out of him. Amusement! bah! Information! chit! He has none to give but on the one point, and surely that old gentleman cannot be interesting himself in the Count's affairs. No matter! I'll see to-morrow!"

Monsieur Leroux was every bit as much put out as the innkeeper of the Villa del Reale. He had no doubt whatever that Matteo had come to the "Golden Bush" designedly. Giovanni had acknowledged that he was an old acquaintance, and, as Leroux turned the subject over in his mind, it began to dawn upon him that this matter might also have some relation with the brigands. He had little doubt but that Patroceni had numbers of spies in Naples devoted to his interests. To get at the bulk of these would require more time than he could devote to it. He must strike hard and strike quickly, or it would be too late. Men with the halters round their necks resent any dallying about their release, and Leroux felt pretty sure that before many days that ransom would be paid; and, let Patroceni only once receive that money, his prisoners would be set free, and he and his band dispersed through the length and breadth of the land. Matteo was at the " Golden Bush " in good time the next day. He picked out a retired table in a far-away corner, boldly ordered his *déjeuner*, and, producing a newspaper, pretended to be immersed in its contents. But for all that, never a soul that entered the tavern escaped his observation. He had not to wait very long before Giovanni appeared, and made his way to the table he had yesterday occupied with the air of an *habitué*. He took no notice of Matteo, but having seated himself was apparently awaiting the arrival of some friend before ordering his repast. The innkeeper had little doubt as to who that friend was, nor was he kept much longer in ignorance of the point. A very few minutes, and Leroux entered the room, and proceeded quietly across to Giovanni's table; but the man's eye was like a hawk's, and, though neither glance nor manner proclaimed it, he had taken in Matteo's presence before he had advanced six steps over the threshold of the room.

"Your old friend apparently takes a great interest in your welfare," said Leroux, quietly, as he seated himself at the table. " Well, that is nice; our old friends as a rule are apt to trouble their heads very little about what becomes of us."

"I don't understand you, signor; what on earth do you mean?"

"Mean!" retorted the police-agent. "Only that your friend—ah! I forget now what you call him; but our excellent host of the Pavilion is breakfasting here. Had you not better ask him to join us?"

"What!" growled Giovanni, with evident perturbation of manner, "Matteo here! Where?"

"Keep quiet," said Leroux; "what is there surprising in that? The best inn-keeper in the city may tire of his own wine at times, and long for a little change. It is only when you get to my age one becomes conservative and runs in grooves."

"Matteo here!" muttered the bandit; "where?"

"As I thought," said Leroux to himself. "Evidently one of Patroceni's auxiliaries.

My friend here, I am afraid, is a little in awe of him. He is sitting over in that corner," he added, aloud; "hadn't you better go over and ask him to join us?"

"Matteo here! Santo Diavolo! Does he suppose I'll submit to his playing the spy upon me?"

"Tut, tut, signor! it is absurd to think anything of that sort; pray go across and ask your friend to join us. His presence here is, doubtless, a mere chance."

"He is afraid of this man's surveillance," muttered Leroux, as the brawny bandit rose from his chair and crossed the room to where Matteo was seated. "This innkeeper of the Pavilion is, doubtless, one of Patroceni's most trusted agents. Quite as well I discovered this. I must study this man closely. From the little I've seen of him I can fancy him one of the Count's shrewdest partisans. This was what made him hover round our table so in the Villa del Reale, and that is what makes my black-bearded friend

so uncommonly uneasy now. A past master
this," thought Leroux, while his lips curled,
" of whom the Signor Giovanni is much
afraid."

But things apparently were not going
quite amicably at Matteo's table. It was
evident that Giovanni was using rough language, and equally transparent that Matteo
was deprecating his wrath. The bandit
indeed had roughly told his old comrade
that he would submit to no dogging of his
footsteps in this wise, that he was in Naples
for his own convenience, that he was on no
duty this time, and that it was nothing to
Matteo, his Excellency, or any one else, how
he passed his time. In vain the supple innkeeper deprecated his anger, and vowed that
his appearance at the " Golden Bush " was
the veriest of accidents. Giovanni's ire was
not to be appeased, and the growling of the
storm bid fair to attract the attention of the
room, when Herr Stein glided across and
poured oil on the troubled waters.

"You will come across, signor," he said, "and eat your meal with us, I am sure: it is better so, and this little matter of politics about which you appear to be differing can be amicably discussed over a glass of wine."

Giovanni stared at his new friend in blank amazement. Politics forsooth! it was no matter of politics that lay between him and Matteo. Men had persecuted each other on the Italian Peninsula pretty bitterly on that point, but it was a bigger difference than that which stood between him and Matteo. A personal vendetta, that, whatever the innkeeper might think about it, was only to be atoned for in Giovanni's thinking by blood; and, as if his scheming comrade had not wrought him bitter wrong enough, here was he once more playing the spy upon him in Naples.

Did Matteo suppose that he (Giovanni) was a mere child under his pupilage? That he was to be watched, treated, and punished like a schoolboy ? And then he ground his teeth as he thought to no schoolboy had punishment ever been meted out so cruel as his.

It was not altogether a pleasant party. Leroux exerting himself to the utmost, was the pleasant, talkative, elderly man of the world. Matteo, silky and subtle, did his very best to respond ; but Giovanni, in his brooding sullenness, hung like a pall over his companions. He drank, and drank deeply, in gloomy silence. No sally of his companions could bring a smile to his swart, saturnine face. He was brooding over his wrongs and taking thought about the righting of them; and when a man in these southern countries dreams about righting his wrongs with his own right hand there is wont to be a vista of blood in the background of the picture.

CHAPTER III.

DEATH OF MATTEO.

It was early morning, the working world of Naples was just beginning to bestir itself, when two or three of those first afoot were disappointed at finding the Pavilion not as yet opened. Matteo, too, was a man with the character of having his shutters down betimes. Rather a popular resort in which to get an early cup of coffee or glass of spirits. The early comers growled their disappointment, and proceeded in search of their needs elsewhere. But, as the sun rose higher in the heavens, the closed door and windows began to attract more attention.

A house of call unexpectedly closed is sure to provoke notice, and the Pavilion did a good deal of business in its way. Some of the would-be customers now drummed boldly on the door, and shouted loudly to Matteo to come forth and attend to their requirements; but the innkeeper made no sign. Nothing but an impenetrable silence responded to their cries.

At this juncture the man who habitually assisted Matteo in the business made his appearance. Failing to get an answer to his shouts for admittance he went round the building to see if he could obtain admission at the back. But no! that door was as securely fastened as the front. The waiter explained that he lived at home with his family, and always returned to them in the evening, coming the first thing in the morning, and having his meals in the Pavilion. It does not take much to excite the curiosity of one's fellow-creatures, and a perfect volley of questions was put to the waiter by the little knot now gathered about the building. He had wished Matteo "Good night" about ten; the innkeeper had told him not to fasten the front door, as, though all the guests had gone, he expected a visitor. The housekeeper, who slept in the upper rooms, had gone to bed some time before he left. It was very odd; neither Matteo nor the woman-servant were given to over-sleeping themselves; such a thing had never happened before in all his recollection, and he had been there for the last two years; he thought something must have happened. Had they not better break in the door?

That the door had better be broken in was carried unanimously, as it was sure to be. A curious crowd will invariably vote for the clearing up of a mystery; but when it came to who was to do it then the little knot were not so positive: each being apparently of the opinion that this was a duty that it behoved his neighbour to undertake rather than himself. There was

much discussion on this point—dexterous
appeals made to individual vanities on the
subject: whereas it was pointed out to one
that his physical strength would make the
breaking of a door open an easy matter to
him, so was it suggested to another that his
well-known knowledge of locks indicated
him as a fitting person to break down the
barrier. But Matteo was known to have a
will of his own; he was known also to keep
lethal weapons on the premises, and was
likely to resent intrusion on his privacy
somewhat sharply. Moreover, the authorities had strong opinions about breaking
into houses in Naples. Then the little
crowd jumped to a conclusion, as such
assemblies are wont to do when wanting
to see what is behind a locked door, but
quite declining to take the responsibility of
forcing the lock. It became necessary to
fix that duty upon somebody. Clearly the
waiter was the man, and shrilly the crowd
clamoured that he should do his *devoir*.

But Carlo, the waiter in question, demurred; he pointed out that his master was a peremptory man who endured no nonsense; that when you forced a man's front door he was justified in the use of either pistol or poignard; that he valued his skin; that, moreover, his master might give him in charge to the police.

"The police! the police! That's it," shouted the mob. " You've hit it, my little man. Of course, it's their business. What are they for but to look into matters like this? Send for the police! Fetch the police somebody!" And then once more, with charming unanimity, the little knot of gossip-mongers cried out to the waiter to fetch the police.

Carlo, only too well pleased to be out of the affair in this fashion, was about to start, best pace, for the bureau, when the attention of all was arrested by a wild, melancholy wail that came from within the closed house. The men exchanged looks

with each other. "Holy Virgin! What
does it mean?" cried some, and then faces
became awed, as men's do who feel themselves on the threshold of viewing a great
tragedy.

Once again came that prolonged dolorous
cry, and a slight shiver ran through the
group as Antonio, the locksmith, murmured
in awe-stricken tones, "*It's his dog.* There
is death in the house, or the dumb creature
would never send forth such a pitiful cry of
dismay. Depend upon it, friends, Matteo
will never loose cork for us more."

The howl of the dog and the exhortations
of the bystanders lent a strong impetus to
Carlo's feet, and he sped away for the
bureau of police as fast as they could carry
him. It was not likely the heads of the
office were going to be bothered about the
keeper of a second-class tavern not getting
up in the morning. Bah! The man had
probably taken more than was good for him
overnight, and was simply sleeping off the

fumes of it. If they were to be called upon to interfere about every one who chose to lie a-bed in Naples they would have enough to do. Still Carlo looked so frightened that, after grumbling a good deal, they finally despatched a gendarme with him.

Supported by this authority, Signor Antonio, the locksmith, speedily undertook to force the door. He had not much difficulty with the lock, but the door was another matter. He quickly ascertained that a heavy wooden bar—dropped, no doubt, into stanchions—prohibited entry as well. Of course, it was possible to cut a panel and withdraw this bar, but it would take time. Before doing so, Antonio suggested they should try some other ingress. Possible, for instance, that the back door, though locked, was not defended by bolts and bars. Antonio marched round at the head of the little company, and commenced operations on the rear of the premises. Here he was very soon successful, the lock quickly

yielded to his efforts, and there were no
further defences to hinder an entrance.

Accompanied by the gendarme and waiter,
the locksmith entered the narrow passage,
and gazed about him. The plan of the little
house was simple in the extreme. Entering
from the back on the right of the narrow
passage which ran straight through it was
the kitchen, and in front of that a small
parlour, on the left a scullery, fronted again
by a comfortable bar. Above the parlour
was the guest-chamber. Over the bar was
Matteo's own bedroom, while at the back
on the upper story were a couple of small
servants' rooms. There was an odour of
crime in the air, when once again came
forth that dolorous howl from a room in
the upper story. Three paces, and the
locksmith started back, and with an exclamation of horror pointed to the foot of
the stairs. Weltering in her blood across
the two bottom steps lay Nita, the housekeeper, a powerful woman of thirty, but

who, it was too palpable, would never dress
macaroni or toss an omelette again. For
the first time the gendarme, who had so far
been stolidly phlegmatic in his movements,
and evidently looked upon the whole affair
as utterly beneath his notice, woke up and
gave signs of animation. Turning rapidly
round he sharply forbade further intrusion
on the part of the crowd, who were following
at his heels; he would have the locksmith,
Carlo, and no other. Stooping down he
roughly raised the woman's hand and convinced himself that she was dead. He then
pushed on and peeped in at the bar. It
had evidently never been closed for the
night; the room was open, glasses stood
about, and half-filled decanters. He next
opened the door of the little parlour to the
right, and there lay the body of the luckless
Matteo, with his face beaten nearly out of
all recognition. That Matteo had fought
hard for his life was evident; the table was
upturned, there was a *débris* of broken

glass, and also a chair in like case, while the clots of blood with which the room was stained gave evidence of a dire struggle between Matteo and his murderer. That the innkeeper had neither physical courage nor strength has been already mentioned, but the old proverb of the " rat in the corner " may usually be counted on. Old men, and men by no means remarkable for courage, have died wondrous hard, very much to the astonishment of their murderers, before now.

Life is sweet and not parted with willingly, as a rule. The gendarme rose rapidly to the occasion; he was in the presence of a great crime, and was not going to bate one bit of his official importance under such circumstances. A discovery of this kind is as the find is to the fox-hunter. Everybody without exception was peremptorily ordered out of the house, and, having closed the door, the gendarme quietly told Carlo to go back to the bureau as fast as he could,

acquaint them there with what he had seen,
and say that he (Pedrillo) had remained in
charge of the building. The police-agent
Leroux happened to be in the chief's office
when this intelligence arrived. He left the
questioning of Carlo to his superior, remain-
ing himself taciturn as usual, but not a
word escaped him, and already his active
brain was piecing the puzzle together. He
had made up his mind that Giovanni was at
least in connection with the bandits; he and
Matteo were evidently old friends, and he
suspected in consequence that Matteo also
was connected with them; that there was
bad blood between the two men had been
palpable at the "Golden Bush" the day
before; that Giovanni had resented his comrade's appearance there; and, rightly or
wrongly, attributed it to a desire to pry
into his (Giovanni's) movements. "Now,"
thought Leroux, "only let Signor Matteo
have got it into his head that my burly,

black-headed friend was coqueting with the
police, and let him know that he thought
so, and I can fancy in a combined fit of
rage and terror his committing just such a
crime as this. These messieurs of the mountain side are pretty prompt and ruthless in
their treatment of traitors, I've heard, and
Giovanni would know. Let them but once
think he even dreamt of betraying them, his
life would not be safe outside Naples. He
was a keen, shrewd man, that innkeeper,
and, if my surmise is just, he let Giovanni
know that he had some suspicion of the
truth."

However, while Leroux is running all
these things over in his mind, the chief of
the police has elicited all Carlo has to tell,
and, turning round to Leroux, suggests that
he should go down and make a preliminary
examination, to which of course Leroux at
once assents.

When he arrives at the Pavilion he finds

it surrounded by a considerable crowd.
The intelligence of the double murder has
spread through the city, gathering size like
a snowball as it rolled ; a whole family has
been murdered, and the numoers of that
family progress in proportion to the number
of times the tale is told. People flocked to
see the scene of the tragedy, although so
far it consists in simply gazing at the outside walls of a closed house; for Pedrillo
stands sentry at the one door that has
been forced, and sternly refuses permission
for even so much as a peep at the interior.
Leroux says a few brief words to his followers, and the gendarmes, in obedience to
his directions, form a cordon round the
building. He then enters, followed only by
Carlo and Pedrillo, whom he orders to stand
perfectly still and to touch nothing. Leroux's first proceeding is to undo all the
shutters with his own hand, carefully noticing the fastenings as he did so, to see

if they had been tampered with. A question to Carlo confirms his idea that the back door was unbolted and unbarred when they forced its lock. No doubt the assassin or assassins entered that way, re-locking the door behind them when they had accomplished their hideous work. Leroux next enters the parlour: there he stands motionless, while his eyes rove rapidly round the room. He glances down at the dead man, and peers keenly into the battered countenance. Not quite an ordinary murder this, he thinks. Whoever slew this man bore him undying hate, hate so strong that he vented his rage on him after he had killed him. The innkeeper was dead when some of those blows were rained upon his mutilated face. The tables are all upset, and the glasses broken now; but there must have been a festive meeting before the wild beast flew at his prey. Signor Matteo could have little dreamt his life was in danger, or he would have never given spirits to such a man as Giovanni. It was the match to the gunpowder; it was letting the tiger taste blood.

Then he quietly left the room and closed the door behind him. He regarded the dead woman at the foot of the staircase narrowly. "No hate here," he muttered; "she has been slain with two strokes of a poignard. Ah! and, as I thought, here is the upturned candlestick. Killed, poor woman, because she at the sound of the disturbance was rash enough to come downstairs and become a witness to the murder. Yes," he continued to himself, as he examined the passage, "here is the first splash of blood; and here is the candle. She came upon him just as he had slain Signor Matteo. He flew at her, struck her in the passage first, and then hunted her to the foot of the stairs, where he dealt the second blow, which killed her. It's all clear as noon-day," thought the police-agent; " the poor creature was trying to escape upstairs when her fate overtook her." Leroux next went into the bar. He looked at the decanters and half-emptied glasses, and muttered to himself with a half smile,

"My bandit friend doubtless manufactured himself a pretty stiff sedative before taking his departure; " and then the police-agent, being careful to move nothing, commenced a close and thorough search of the house. But he found nothing by which to trace the murderer. There was not a button, not a shred of clothes, nor anything by which to identify the assassin, left behind, and as far as the police-agent could ascertain no property had been taken from the house.

As he opened the servant's bedroom at the back of the house a small dog, evidently half-wild with fright, sprang back from the door and snarled at him in the

madness of its terror. But no sooner were
they well inside the attic than it made one
sudden dart through them, and almost fell
from the top to the bottom of the stairs in
its agony to escape. The demented little
thing made at once for the front door,
which, as it knew, in the usual state of
things would be open by that time. Suddenly it stopped transfixed in front of the
dead body of the servant. The ghastly
scent of blood, and the presence of death,
thoroughly upset the remainder of its bewildered ideas. It uttered one prolonged
melancholy howl, and then, catching sight
of the open backdoor, fled through the
portal like a mad creature—dumb witness
concerning a murder about which there was
none else to testify.

Leroux ordered the house to be again
locked up, placed a guard over it, and
walked back to the bureau to give orders
about the usual legal preliminaries.

" I have very little doubt," he muttered to himself, " as to who the real criminal is, but there's not a particle of evidence against him; and, what is more, with a view to settling with messieurs les brigands *en bloc*, I require my decoy-duck to retain his liberty for a little longer."

CHAPTER IV.

AT THE GOLDEN BUSH.

THERE was perhaps no man in Naples so
perturbed at Matteo's murder as Fred Hammerton. He had no doubt whatever about
the innkeeper of Villa del Reale's connection with Patroceni. As he listened to the
accounts of the tragedy he became assured
that this was an act of savage vengeance;
and that it had been perpetrated at the
instigation of the Count, and no doubt in
consequence of suspected treachery on the
part of Matteo. It may be remembered
that Hammerton had recognised the unfortunate man, and hailed him when he had

E 2

passed their carriage on the way to Amalfi.
Hammerton had caught sight of him afterwards in the brigands' camp; and it was
quite clear to him that the slain innkeeper
had done them the honour that day to be
their *avant courier*. He felt quite sure that
it was Matteo who had given due notice of
their speedy arrival at the foot of that
forest-fringed hill where they had fallen
into the hands of Patroceni. What had
been this man's crime? What had called
forth the fiat that had led to his doom?
Hammerton's experience of these men of
the mountain was extremely limited, and
like most of those whose misfortune it has
been to make their acquaintance he had no
desire to extend it. But he was under a
strong impression that brigandage, like all
other secret societies, lived in constant fear
of betrayal, and consequently never neg-
lected making a terrible example of an
informer. About Matteo's individual fate
Hammerton cared little; but the question

was, if Patroceni feared treachery how
would he treat the prisoners in his hands?
He might connect him—Hammerton—with
the dead man's bad faith. This might
make the Count suspect that he was col-
leaguing with the police, and how he was
to disprove this he did not know. He had
never been near the police, and to the best
of his belief they were unaware of his presence in Naples at this minute. He wondered what it was best for him to do. To
seek for information from the bureau would
probably be a fatal mistake. The Count
had no doubt plenty of well-wishers in
Naples who would speedily acquaint him
should he (Hammerton) put himself into
communication with the authorities. But
then, on the other hand, how on earth was
he now to send note or message to Patroceni? As yet there had been no call to do
so; but it was to this very Matteo he had
been told to apply when he felt that he
had news worth the sending. This crime

had unexpectedly cut him entirely off from
the camp and its inmates. What would
they all think of him up there in the woods,
he muttered; what would Wheldrake think
of him; what would Glanfield say of him.
He had committed a treason at Wrottsley
bad as he could be suspected of committing
now, and had felt little compunction about
it. Yet such was the curious kink in the
man's mind that he shrank from the bare
idea of playing the traitor here. Im-
perfectly as he understood Italian, still he
had gathered enough from Pietro during his
escape to know that Wheldrake—the man
he had so bitterly injured—had probably
risked his own life to save his. Sensualist,
sybarite, and gambler as he was, Hammerton was touched by this, and he swore a big
oath on his way to Naples to do the best
he could according to his lights in this
matter; yes, even in case of the worst, to
go back to the camp and to share in the
fate of the rest of them. It was hard upon

him : he had nothing to do with it; it was
the sheer force of adverse circumstances.
He had kept closely to himself since his
arrival in the city, and been reticent and
self-constrained in the extreme ; and yet,
though he did not know it, he was in
communication with the police, and had
indirectly contributed to the murder of
Matteo.

Hammerton had a big smoke as he pondered over all this ; but, for the life of him,
he could see nothing to do at present but
sit still and await the course of events.

Police-agent Leroux was quite as much
put out in his calculations by this murder
as the Captain. He similarly doubted
whether his communication with the camp
was not also cut off. Matteo, it is true,
had nothing to say to the conveyance of his
letters thereto; but the question was,
whether this human tiger he employed had
not, his passion satiated, fled back to his
haunts on the mountain-side after the

manner of his four-footed type upon the conclusion of a successful foray. He had no doubt whatever that Giovanni was the murderer, and he knew that men of that class, when their hands are red, are rather given to seek safety in flight. Leroux felt no doubt about laying his hands upon Giovanni whenever he wanted him; but at present his principal anxiety was that he should not leave Naples. The police-agent had hit upon a very crafty scheme for successfully surprising Patroceni; but it all depended upon his keeping touch with the camp, and without Giovanni's assistance he did not well know how this was to be done. Well! it was a problem soon solved. He had but to make up as Herr Stein, and drop in for his noon-day meal as usual at the "Golden Bush."

In spite of being harassed with numerous details concerning Matteo's murder he succeeded about the accustomed time in making his appearance at the quiet little tavern, and the first thing that met his view after entering was the burly brigand sipping wine and munching bread while waiting for the repast he had ordered.

Giovanni stretched out his hand to Leroux in boisterous welcome. There was even a triumphant sparkle in his eyes, as those of a man to whom good luck has come.

"Ah, my friend," he exclaimed, "I am glad to see you this morning, for I've a famous appetite. We'll have a flask of the best to wash down the pigeons and macaroni that I have ordered."

"The brute finds killing a hungry occupation," thought Leroux, as he shook hands. "However, his nerves seem of iron, and he exhibits no tendency to fly the city, and that suits my purpose. Good morning!" he continued, aloud, "I should have been here sooner but I was so interested in this terrible murder that has been committed—a murder that concerns you in some measure."

"Concerns me?" growled Giovanni.
"You don' suppose I had anything to do
with it?"

Leroux glanced at him as a cat might at
a mouse.

"Ah," he said carelessly, "you have
heard of the tragedy, then?"

"Yes; I heard something about it," rejoined the bandit.

"There can be very little doubt about his
guilt," thought Leroux. "A man who had
just heard of the murder of an old friend
would be full of the subject, and commence
talking of it at once. No," he continued
aloud, "I am not hinting that; but, as the
unfortunate man was an old ally of yours, I
thought you might have been painfully
interested in his fate."

"We were old acquaintances, and had
business relations," replied Giovanni, sulkily.
"He sold bad liquor and charged me dear
for it."

"A too common offence," replied Leroux,

gravely, "not often meeting with such terrible punishment as it has in this case."

"Don't talk of it," rejoined Giovanni. "I heard somebody he had wronged had beaten the fellow to death. I've no doubt he deserved it."

"A very singular crime," observed the police-agent, musingly. "They tell me that the house is a perfect shambles. The assassin has killed not only Signor Matteo but his cook also, and so far there seems no conjecture, even, as to who he was or what was his motive."

"Ah," said Giovanni, "they suspect no one, eh?"

"No one," answered Leroux. "What the police may think they will doubtless keep to themselves. By the way, I have another note that I want forwarded to the camp, just to say that the raising of the money is nearly completed. This gentleman who has been released is very anxious to let his friends know that."

Giovanni extended his hand for the letter, and glanced greedily at the gold pieces that accompanied it. For a moment they absorbed all his attention, but as he put the letter into his pocket he noticed that it was fastened.

" This is closed," he exclaimed. " What does that mean ? " And as he asked the question he glanced suspiciously at the police-agent.

" Stupid of him ! " replied Leroux, carelessly. " I told him always to send his letters open. You had better give me both that and the money back, and I will bring you another to-morrow; it is a pity, as the signor was very anxious to send off his news at once."

Giovanni hesitated; he was loth to part with the gold, and yet extremely anxious not to do anything that could do harm to his comrades. He sat playing with the money and turning the whole thing over in his mind, and at length it dawned upon him that after all he had known nothing of the contents of the previous notes he had forwarded beyond what Leroux had told him.

"I will do it," he said at last. "The contents are what you tell me?"

"What else should he have to write about?" inquired Leroux, jesuitically, and gold and letter at once disappeared into the bandit's pocket.

Now, there was in that note what Leroux had stated; but when he asked what else could the signor have to say he knew very well that it also contained news of the murder.

Chisel had been very much surprised when Herr Stein had come to him in a great hurry that morning, and made him add to his usual report that things were progressing as favourably as possible these few lines:—"An innkeeper called Matteo, who kept the Pavilion in the Villa del

Reale, was brutally murdered last night."
The police-agent thought that the captives
should be furnished with this piece of intelligence, which might possibly be the
cause of some menace to their lives. Police-
agent Leroux was quite convinced that the
crafty, subtle, innkeeper had been an agent
of Patroceni's; and, from all he had ever
heard of the Count, thought that he was
just the man to avenge the death of one of
his instruments. If the Count was only
aware that the murder had been committed
by one of his own people, then, of course,
it was a matter amongst the bandits themselves, but there was nothing to show
that.

Leroux at this time was under a like
excitement that attends the sportsman in
the middle of a big run. He had, as far as
he could see, all the strings of the game in
his hand; and, though he by no means
overlooked the fact that he had a great man

against him, and all the more dangerous
because nothing had been heard of him
lately, still he did think that he should
checkmate Count Patroceni in the course of
a few days. Chisel, who writes these notes,
has no idea that they are dictated by the
police; but is under the impression that
they proceed from Herr Stein himself, who
has pointed out to him that, as a great
financial agent, he has several times had
the arranging of these things, and so has
his own way of communicating with the
fraternity of the mountains. Thus it is
always best to keep the captives constantly
informed that every nerve is being strained
to procure the necessary money; it re-
assures the brigands, and makes them feel
that the authorities are not being invoked
to their detriment. Leroux is planning a
very daring *coup*, and at present he is not
a little troubled as to whether Matteo's
murder may affect his combinations. It

has already made so much stir in the city
that there can be little doubt of the intelligence very speedily reaching Patroceni's
ears, and, as the police-agent shrewdly
guessed, the loss of a trusted confederate in
Naples might alter the Count's proceedings
in many ways.

In spite of all his astuteness, Leroux had
not got as much out of Giovanni as he
expected. This was due partly to the
police-agent's fears of pushing his questioning too far, and thereby scaring so shy a
fish, and partly to Giovanni having had
some reticence literally knocked into his
head. The operation might have been
severe, but it had undoubtedly been effec-
tual, and Giovanni was now very guarded
when speaking of the Count. Leroux was
right in one conjecture; intelligence of the
murder speedily reached the · camp, but,
beyond Pietro, no one had the slightest idea
of the truth. As for the Count, he was not

even aware that Giovanni was alive; he had never seen him since he struck him down, nor had he been told of his recovery. Pietro alone, of all the bandits, was aware of the revengeful feelings Giovanni had entertained towards the dead man.

CHAPTER V.

PATROCENI PUZZLED.

WHEN Wheldrake got Chisel's note telling him of the murder he at once showed it to Glanfield, and the two commenced to talk the matter over.

"I don't see," he observed, "how this can affect our business, but it may; this man I know is connected with the brigands —indeed, he had much to do with my own capture. As you know, I was kidnapped at his house; and I heard him give evidence before the Count as to a ruffian called Giovanni's drunkenness. It was to this Giovanni that I owe being made prisoner.

In his cups I drew him out as to what Patroceni was; and the Count told me himself that I might thank my thirst for knowledge for bringing me here. I had learnt too much to be left at liberty."

" I can hardly say I have seen this innkeeper," replied Glanfield. " A horseman passed us on the road just before we fell in with our friends here, and Hammerton told me afterwards it was the proprictor of the Pavilion. As for this Giovanni, I have never seen him at all."

" And are never likely to do so now," interposed Wheldrake. " Patroceni, as a punishment for his intoxication, dealt him a blow with the butt-end of his pistol that I should think sent him straight to the other world. At all events, he was carried away for dead."

" Well," replied Glanfield, " we can't be suspected of having anything to do with it. It is a clear *alibi* for all of us except Hammerton; and, though I look upon him as quite capable of snatching at anything in the way of money, I don't think he is likely to go in for murdering an innkeeper. Some of that man Giovanni's relations, I should think, have settled an old score against Matteo. They would, doubtless, hear that he had caused the death of their interesting relation."

"Everything seems going on all right according to this," said Wheldrake, as he once more glanced at Chisel's note, " but they are excessively slow. I suppose Hammerton is really doing his best ?"

"As I said before," rejoined Glanfield, " when they've once run rogues never stand them again, but I believe he is running straight this time. Remember, this is a country where they always take plenty of time to do everything. That raising money at very short notice means paying proportionately long interest. I once heard a great financial agent accustomed to finding the means for many a black Monday, say,

—when two of his clients of the plunging school had run a dead-heat, and, not content with the very heavy stakes they had had in the first go, backed their opinions again with renewed obstinacy,—I heard him say, on being appealed to as to which he thought would win the decider,—'Don't ask me, I shall have ten thousand to find on Monday whichever way it is, and that is enough for me to think about!'"

"A very instructive anecdote, Glanfield," said Sir Jasper, laughing, who had approached them unobserved just in time to catch this little illustration. "I recollect the case; and, if such an expert as you are alluding to thought there would be a difficulty in getting that sum in London for two such clients as his, we can't expect but that in Naples the difficulties of raising such a much larger amount will be very much greater. We have seen nothing of our host, Mr. Wheldrake, since you interfered with his arrangements."

This was a sort of extension of the olive-branch on Sir Jasper's part. He was willing to treat Wheldrake somewhat more cordially than he had done of late. The *gutta cavat lapidem* had gradually told upon Sir Jasper. His daughter, his sister, and Glanfield persistently affirmed Wheldrake's innocence; and, though he was not convinced, nor the least reconciled to the idea of any marriage between Maude and Wheldrake, still he wished for past times to be on a more friendly footing with the young man.

But Cyril had no idea of resuming relations with the baronet on that platform. He could not pretend to be on amicable terms with one who could entertain such a doubt of his honour as Sir Jasper made no scruple of admitting still possessed him, and his response was cold and measured.

"You do not approve of my tactics, Sir Jasper. I am sorry for it. Much more satisfactory to you, I should have thought, than the business resting in my hands."

The baronet immediately drew himself up. He was not prepared to find his overtures so coldly responded to. His observation had been simply the prelude to more genial converse than had passed between them of late; but it was very possible for a proud man like Wheldrake to interpret it as a sarcastic gibe at his having interfered at all in the ordering of things.

"Our worthy friends here were on the drink again last night, so Jackson tells me," observed the baronet, quietly ignoring Wheldrake's reply. "I should think, like the Saxons, they would awake to their Hastings some fine morning. If the Neapolitan police had the slightest enterprise they would find very little difficulty in capturing these fellows."

"Then all I can say is it is devoutly to be hoped they will continue to want enterprise," said Glanfield. "I take it to capture Patroceni and our friends here is a cut above any man they have got amongst them. I

fancy that these beggars would fight under
the Count, and that moreover as a preliminary his Excellency would shoot the balance
of his prisoners."

"What! supposing that an attack took
place upon him from no breach of faith on
our part?" said Sir Jasper.

"You see he would not have time to look
into that. We should find ourselves in the
forfeit list and struck out of all engagements."

"We must take our chance," said Sir
Jasper. "But the carelessness of the look-
out kept by these fellows absolutely invites
a police raid on the place. They might have
Patroceni and all these fellows bound and
trussed like turtles without firing a shot or
losing a life.

"Now, baronet," said Glanfield, laughing,
"I know where your inspiration comes from.
I can see old Jackson's finger all through
that idea. That blessed old idiot only sees
one-half of the question. He sees a good

many of these fellows swallow a lot of wine, and lie down to sleep. But they are a long way off the intoxicated state he imagines them in; while their sentries, although they don't act like regular soldiers, have got their eyes pretty widely open. I've wandered about the camp at all hours, and know it. Take my word, if the police make a dash at our friends here, you'll see an uncommon pretty fight—that is, should the Count not resort to that preliminary measure I think probable."

Sir Jasper said nothing; he was so weary of inaction that had he not been hampered by his daughter and sister he would have urged a dash for freedom in the teeth of the cooler counsels of Jim Glanfield. "I suppose there is no further news from Naples?" he inquired at last.

"Yes; Wheldrake heard everything was going on all right this morning; but it is a tedious business."

Glanfield did not think it necessary to

mention anything about Matteo's murder to the baronet. He had no knowledge of the innkeeper, and it would, therefore, interest him but little. Nor was it easy to see how it concerned any of them. Yet Wheldrake had seemed to think it might.

Here Maude and Mrs. Fullerton interrupted the conversation.

"We are discussing, Mr. Glanfield," said the vivacious widow, "the charms of this mountain residence; it was delightful at first,"—a savage grunt of dissent from Sir Jasper,—"but it is beginning to get a wee bit monotonous now. We pine for our maids, and I am sure you must all be as tired of our gowns as we are."

"The circumstances are trying, but I shall always stick to it that you are the best ——"

"No, Mr. Glanfield, I won't have it," interposed Mrs. Fullerton, quietly. "I know exactly what you are going to say. Best anything you like, but *not groomed*."

"Best turned-out woman I know."

"That's painfully true," replied Mrs. Fullerton, gravely. "Very much turned out, Maude dear, are we not? But it's on the mountain-side and a good many miles from civilisation. You need not mock us for all that. I know I'm a perfect guy, but you can't expect a woman to be anything else whose maid is leagues away from her. Do you think we shall have to stay here much longer?"

"I was just telling Sir Jasper that Wheldrake's latest news is that everything is progressing favourably. But we can learn nothing more definite than that."

"It really is to be hoped," said Maude, "that our captivity will not last very much longer. It is getting very awkward in the matter of dress, you know."

"Really," rejoined Glanfield, laconically; "had to wash my own shirt yesterday, you know, and I can't say it does me credit. Looks worse than when I began."

Matteo's tragical end had affected Patroccni in a way neither Leroux nor Hammerton had foreseen. The Count was puzzled; he had no theory whatever as to the cause of the crime. He most certainly did not suspect Hammerton, nor was it possible for him to suspect the real culprit, whom he did not even know to be alive. With what object had the innkeeper been assassinated? Obviously not for plunder, for his informants were very precise on that point, saying that no property of any kind had been touched. The Count was considerably put out about it, if only for this reason: Matteo was one of the shrewdest and most trusted agents he had in the city, one whom it would be hard to replace. That it could mean any menace to himself he thought very improbable; but the Count was much too old and practised not to be suspicious of even a chance blow aimed at one of his instruments. He did not understand this, and, like most men whose lot it has been to be much hunted, had more dread of the mysterious than clearly defined danger. He had received no certain news from Hammerton about the ransom as yet. Hammerton indeed had only sent one communication through Matteo, which had been pretty much to the same effect as those that Leroux had despatched in Chisel's writing to Wheldrake, namely, that all arrangements were made, but must take a few days to conclude.

" It is no use," mused Patroceni, " and there is no one I can trust. I have no one with brains enough to look into this thing for me. I must know why one of my emissaries is slain. Half my power round Naples would be gone if it was not known that it is dangerous to meddle with Patroceni's followers. If the police don't find Matteo's murderer *I will*. He'll fare no better in my hands than in theirs, and probably make a much quicker ending of it. No. There's only one thing for it, I must go into Naples myself. I'll start at daybreak to-morrow morning."

This was not so hazardous as it might sound. It has been before remarked that the Count was a man cunning in disguise. He had gone freely about the city under divers personations; but it was only of late that he and his followers had taken refuge in the woods above Amalfi, and it was only their last exploit that had attracted the attention of the police to their being there. During the two or three previous years, the Count and his followers had infested districts somewhat remote from Naples, and had only migrated upon finding they had made those districts too hot to hold them. The Count had always had his spies in Naples—indeed, he had spies pretty generally through the country. Many of these were his old political associates, who still kept up brisk communication with each other with the hope that the whirligig of time might bring to them another chance of snatching at the supreme power; and all of these recognised his Excellency as one of the most sagacious and daring leaders they had; so that between his brigandage and his Carbonari-ism the Count was kept well informed of what went on in most of the leading cities of Italy.

That Patroceni, if recognised, would be arrested, need scarcely be said; but the Count had quite as much confidence in his powers of impersonation as Leroux, and had more than once smoked his cigarette under the noses of the police, with a handsome reward offered for his apprehension. The Count was a man of decision—no sooner had he made up his mind than he sent for his lieutenant.

"Sarini," he said, as that worthy limped into the tent, "I must know the rights of Matteo's death. I intend that whoever took his life shall pay for it with his own. Nothing but fear of swift retribution keeps people loyal to us. We have to trust those

who would sell us if they dared. I shall go
into Naples myself, and see what I can
make of it."

"Will it not be dangerous, Eccellenza,
after our recent capture?"

"I don't think, my old comrade," rejoined
Patroceni, with a sarcastic smile, "that
either you or I ever recked much of that.
You will stay here in command, and I
know I can trust you, if anything happens
to me, to exact retribution for it."

"Most assuredly. Let me hear that you
are a prisoner, and your release shall be the
condition of our captives' freedom; let me
hear of your death and I will shoot them
every one, women and all, with my own
hand. I've followed you now, through
storm and sunshine, for twenty-five years.
You need not fear but what I'll stand to
you still."

"No, my old comrade," rejoined the
Count, and as he spoke there was a gleam
of softness, rarely seen in Patroceni's keen,

cold eyes. "I know I can trust you; you are true as steel. It is not very likely that I shall fall into the hands of the police. If I do, you must do the best you can for me; but at all events insist upon having a note in my handwriting before you come to terms. Don't be precipitate; but, old friend, do not let them send Patroceni across the Styx unattended."

A fierce glance of intelligence flashed across Sarini's face at these words. He, like his chief, was a man of education, and thoroughly understood the allusion.

"Never fear, Eccellenza," he replied. "If it is your fate to take passage in old Charon's boat I'll see that you have company across the river."

CHAPTER VI.

THE DUMB PEDLAR.

THE Golden Bush had no more constant habitués than Giovanni and Herr Stein. To the bandit it represented the principal attraction of his day. To his coarse, sensual nature the chief delights of this world were centered in eating and drinking, and, it may be, gambling, which, now he was in Naples, rather took the form of buying tickets in the lottery. There was no place in which he could indulge the former of these propensities so much at his ease as at this quiet tavern to which the police agent had introduced him. Again, Giovanni had very few acquaintances in Naples, and under the present circumstances shrank from making any. He was not a man, although gregarious in his disposition, likely to attract strangers—far from it. They, as a rule, repelled the advances of the swart, ruffianly-looking bravo. He detested solitude, not that he was suffering in the least from that remorse which is so often pictured to us. An imaginative man of the higher order of intelligence may suffer agonies when in his solitary hours he is brought face to face with the memory of his crime, but the lower organizations of Giovanni's type are no more troubled by such recollections than a wild beast. It was simply that he wearied of his own company, and looked forward to this mid-day meal with Leroux as the pleasantest part of the twenty-four hours. He had no idea at present of leaving the city. He was far too well satisfied with his present quarters, and the money he obtained from

Leroux made it no necessity for him to return to the hill-side. He hated work, but he disliked starvation more, and it was this originally that had been the cause of his turning bandit.

That Leroux should be as constant to their daily tryst as he could manage may easily be conceived. It was his sole opportunity of communicating with the captives; his sole chance of obtaining any information as to what the brigands were about. And the police-agent was wonderfully keen about carrying out a pet scheme of his own, which, should it prove successful, would result in the capture of Patroceni and all his band.

But the best-laid schemes of mice and men, as Burns tells us, often go amiss; and there was this little drawback to Leroux's project—that any failure would probably cost the captives their lives. But the anguine police-agent, although quite aware of this risk, would not permit himself to think of failure, and unluckily did not take

into his counsels those principally concerned.

The pair were seated at their customary
table, and Giovanni in full enjoyment of
his meal.

" I suppose," said Leroux, " you have
got no news for my friend?"

"Not yet," replied Giovanni; "the time
is too short, Signor Stein. They could not
possibly have brought a reply from the
camp by this."

Evident from this speech that Giovanni
has been tolerably confidential of late about
his connection with the brigands. He still
refuses to admit that he is of them, but
makes no secret to his dear friend Signor
Stein that he is on friendly terms with a
good many of them, and knows his Excellency Count Patroceni himself very well.
In good truth he might well say that, being
little likely to forget his Excellency so long
as there is breath in his body. Haughty,
cold, cynical, and stern as the Count habit-

ually was with his followers, there were
times when, like all great commanders, he
would unbend.   Napoleon, when things
went well, would jest with the veterans of
the Grand Army. Patroceni, in like manner,
would occasionally condescend to drink,
smoke, and gamble with his followers ; and,
much as they looked up to him for his
dauntless courage and subtle intellect, it
may be doubted whether they did not hold
him in still higher reverence for his capa-
bilities as a card-player.   When he did join
in the play it was generally a bad time for
his followers.   The Count was one of the
finest artists in Europe at *compelling fortune*
at any game of chance.

"No," rejoined Leroux, "I suppose there
has hardly been time ; but our client, you
see, is anxious. He will have it that the
tragedy in the Villa del Reale may probably
affect the treatment of his friends. It is in
vain I point out to him that the murderer of
that luckless innkeeper can have nothing to

say to Count Patroceni. Quite impossible, don't you think so ?"

"Quite impossible," re-echoed Giovanni; "as if a man like his Excellency would care what happened to such scum as Matteo."

Leroux shot a keen glance at the speaker as he rejoined, "His—ah—what did you call him ?—ah ! Excellency, meaning, I suppose, Count Patroceni, was not likely to know anything of a man like that unfortunate. Still I have heard that these brigand-chiefs have agents under all sorts of disguises. But you know, Signor Giovanni, what tales people will tell of a man like——like his Excellency. By the way, I didn't know that Count Patroceni went by that name."

"Yes, he does, amongst those that serve him. His followers hold him far higher than this new king who has just been pitch-forked on to the throne. I don't understand these things myself, but we all think

his Excellency and his friends are the proper
men to govern us."

"And who are all?" inquired Leroux,
quietly.

Rather an awkward question this. Giovanni was speaking with that laxity characteristic of much higher intelligences than
his own. A tendency to state loosely "that
every one says so," meaning yourself and
about a score of your acquaintances, is a
weakness very prevalent, which has led to
much perversion of history. Leroux's question was an interrogatory eminently calculated to confuse a man like Giovanni.

"All!" he rejoined; "why, everybody!
Who are all? Why, all the people you
meet round about! Why do we call him
his Excellency? Well, because he is his
Excellency. Why do people call you Signor
Stein?"

"Ah, true, true," replied Leroux. "I am
very stupid. We are naturally called by

our names." Or, he thought to himself, "what we give out to be our names; taken, too, in great measure by the world to be what we choose to label ourselves."

"No; his Excellency," resumed Giovanni, "is his Excellency because he was made so in one of these numerous revolts we have had, and which didn't come to anything. I never heard, but 1 daresay they made somebody his Majesty, and if his head is not cut off he is no doubt walking about somewhere. But the Count! Ah! they will never catch him."

"Yes, everybody talks of how clever his Excellency is."

"Clever!" replied Giovanni, in a low whisper; "he could walk straight through the bureau of police without being detected if he pleased. There's nothing he can't do. There's nothing he don't know. And a man's life is not worth a dish of macaroni who falls under his displeasure; and he is merciless, ah! so merciless, when he is offended."

As the last words, uttered in a low tone, escaped the bandit's lips, a pedlar entered the room, and, lifting his pack from off his shoulders, seated himself at a table adjoining,— a well-to-do pedlar apparently, well-clad, and in appearance not of the country. His hair was long and fair, and he wore coloured spectacles, probably on account of some weakness in his eyes; for his lithe wiry figure and general aspect by no means indicated age—a muscular man of medium height, and seemingly in his prime. He summoned the waiter by the simple process of rapping on the table, and having glanced over the bill of fare indicated what he wanted by pointing to it with his finger. Nothing escaped the trained eye of Leroux, and it was hardly likely that he would overlook the preternatural taciturnity of the new comer.

"You have known cases, no doubt, of the Count's relentlessness, Signor Giovanni," observed Leroux, carelessly.

" Known ! " repeated the bandit, who had by this, as usual, consumed a good deal of wine. " I've done more than know; I have seen. You will never mention it again, Signor Stein; but I saw him send a man out of the world one morning for no graver offence than being overpowered with thirst while engaged in his Excellency's business."

" What ! " exclaimed the police-agent, with well-assumed horror; " you surely do not mean that Patroceni slew a man in cold blood merely because he had found the wine-cup too great a temptation ? "

" If he did not kill him," rejoined Giovanni, " it was simply because his day had not come. He was carried away for dead."

" What unheard-of ferocity ! " exclaimed Leroux. " Such an act of cruelty as that is sure to recoil on the perpetrator. I know little of the world, my excellent friend ; but I should imagine that it would be dangerous to Count Patroceni that the victim of such barbarity escaped with his life."

" I don't understand," rejoined Giovanni, curtly.

"Simply this—that resentment of injury is implanted in the breasts of all mankind. Men are apt to be implacable with either undeserved or excessive punishment. A man who had suffered such unheard-of violence for so slight an offence would be dangerously likely to avenge it. Of course," continued Herr Stein, as he threw himself back in his chair and lit a fresh cigarette, " if he were not a man, but simply a cringing spaniel, his submitting to it is easy of comprehension."

Giovanni writhed a little uneasily under the words of this quiet, elderly citizen. The bandit had all the contempt for the dwellers in towns characteristic of the hill-men in all nations, characteristic indeed of the country-people everywhere. Your cockney may look down upon the yokel when he meets him in the streets of the metropolis—he may have the best of it there. Flurried by the crowd and scenes he is unaccustomed to, the countryman in his confusion bows down before the arrogance of his city brother; but, for all that, the denizen of the fields, the man who is face to face with nature, who is conversant with the song of the throstle, with the rustle of the trees and the bloom of the hedges, has in his heart a supreme contempt for the dweller in the city, who knows · nothing about the cheery melody of the hounds, the crack of the breechloader over the autumnal stubbles, or the very meaning of the May-fly being on.

The bandit said nothing; he was slow of thought, and the idea of cherishing resentment against Patroceni had never as yet crossed his mind. He regarded the Count as so far above him that he no more thought of revenging himself for the punishment he had received than a serf would have done

in England in the days of the Saxons. With
his equal like Matteo it had been different;
but his Excellency, ah! their very lives
were in his hands, and yet here was this
quiet, elderly wine-merchant, who apparently
looked upon it that such cruelty would
naturally be resented. He was rather stung
by Leroux's speech, as the crafty police-
agent had intended he should be. He did
not like that this townsman should appear
to think him deficient in spirit, to fancy
that he was a man who submitted meekly
to injuries. Still, the idea that he should
ever have lifted his hand against the Count
seemed preposterous.

Leroux watched him silently : he guessed
pretty well what was passing through Giovanni's mind, and wondered whether it was
possible to blow that spark of resentment,
that he felt he had kindled, into a flame.

"You don't understand," growled the
bandit at last, quite oblivious that he was
admitting that he himself had been the

sufferer. "Giovanni would avenge his wrongs promptly on any other, but with his Excellency our lives are his, to do as he wills with."

At these words Leroux fancied that he saw the pedlar at the adjoining table turn his head towards them. The man had, up to this, been apparently absorbed in his own humble repast, and the police-agent had noticed his extreme taciturnity. The few directions that it was requisite for him to give the waiters he had done by signs. A thought struck Leroux. Suddenly rising from his seat he crossed to the pedlar, and, with a courteous bow, proffered him a cigarette. The man took it, but in answer to Leroux's, "Pray permit me to offer you a cigarette," he expressed his acknowledgment of the civility pantomimically.

Then, seeing the perplexed look on Leroux's face, he shook his head, touched his mouth two or three times with his hand, and again shook his head.

"Why, I believe he is dumb!" exclaimed the police-agent.

As the exclamation escaped him, the pedlar produced a pencil from his vest, and, taking up the bill of fare, hastily scribbled on the back,—"I cannot speak, but am much obliged for your kindness."

Patroceni—for of course it was he—had assumed dumbness the moment he perceived Giovanni. He did not know who the police-agent might be, but he had long since learnt to mistrust all chance acquaintance. Further, there was Giovanni. He had not the slightest fear of that worthy penetrating his disguise, and after his last speech no fear of his intentions of betraying him; but he had no faith in Giovanni's discretion, and thought if the bandit recognised his voice he would show an astonishment that might arouse the attention of the spectators. Another thing, too, that flashed across the Count's mind—Who was this sober-going citizen with whom Giovanni, the hog, had contracted such an apparent intimacy? He knew, none better, what Giovanni was in a social point of view—a dull, stupid drunkard, blindly devoted to him, Patroceni, like a huge mastiff, but without the brute's intelligence. It was hardly likely that a man of some culture, such as the donor of the cigarette undoubtedly was, should think it worth his while to cultivate Giovanni without an object.

Leroux had resumed his seat; the Count smoked on in silence, with his ears keenly alert to catch further conversation; but the talk between the police-agent and his guest languished. It was not that Leroux in the least despaired of gradually inflaming the mind of the bandit against Patroceni, but he saw that it would take more time than he could give to it. The pseudo-pedlar at length picked up his pack, bowed to Leroux, and took his departure.

"A great mistake!" muttered Patroceni,

when he found himself in the street. "Why did I trust to a blow in dealing with such a thick-skulled brute as that? I ought to have shot him, as I originally meant. He is staunch enough at present, but I've no doubt his elderly friend is an emissary of the police. Granting Giovanni remains loyal, as he doubtless intends, it is not difficult to turn a clumsy drunkard like that inside out. I wonder whether that very polite gentleman had the slightest suspicion as to who I really was? As well for him, perhaps, he hadn't; if he were connected with the police he might have made a premature attempt to earn the five hundred pounds offered for my apprehension, which would have resulted in another tragedy in a place of public entertainment. Can Hammerton be playing me false? There's coquetting with the police on the part of some one."

CHAPTER VII.

AN UNWELCOME VISITOR.

THE more he thought over it the more convinced was Patroceni that Giovanni's new
acquaintance had sinister designs of some
sort, and now the Count had the loss of
Matteo at once brought home to him. The
chances were that the dead innkeeper could
have thrown some light upon this mysterious
intimacy—at all events, he was the very
man to discover who was Giovanni's new
friend. True, that was a matter the Count
could clear up for himself; but, for one
thing, he had no intention of being more
than a day in Naples; he had other things

to look to, and he would hardly have the time to make this discovery for himself. And yet, if the police had got hold of Giovanni, the sooner he was ordered back to the mountains the better. A very unsafe adherent, thought the Count, to go through the ordeal of cross-examination. He had been very much astonished at the man's reappearance; neither seeing nor hearing anything of him since he struck him down he had never doubted but that Giovanni was dead; and he could not help thinking that it would have been better if he had never recovered. It was impossible to say what admissions might be drawn from this the very dullest of all his followers. So far the Count's inquiries concerning the death of Matteo had no results; there was no theory as to who the murderer was broached in the city. Conjecture was at fault, and, except Leroux, no one in Naples had a suspicion as to his entity.

The Count was struck with this; he had

expected to find the name of the supposed
assassin in all men's mouths. The story of
the murder undoubtedly was; Carlo had done
nothing but describe the appearance of the
house ever since they broke into it; but as
to who the actual murderer was no one professed knowledge. Still, though there was
nothing to throw light upon Matteo's fate,
the Count thought it just as well that he
had visited the city. There was, very possibly, danger to be feared from Giovanni's
indiscretion, and the sooner that worthy rejoined his comrades the safer it would be
for them all. And then Patroceni made up
his mind that he would call upon Hammerton. He, at all events, would hear
direct how the negotiations for the ransom
were progressing, and would caution the
Captain against any attempt at foul play.

Hammerton's astonishment was considerable when he was informed that there was
somebody wanting to see him. The first in-

quiry was, naturally, as to what manner of man this might be; and, upon being told that he was apparently a Jew pedlar, Hammerton was about promptly to decline the interview when it suddenly occurred to him that this might be a messenger from Patroceni· He had heard nothing from the camp since he left, for he knew nothing of Chisel's correspondence, Leroux having cautioned the valet against showing Wheldrake's notes to any one, pointing out they might cost his master his life should they fall into the hands of the police. So, after turning it over for a minute or two in his own mind, he ordered the stranger to be shown up.

The pedlar made a low bow as he entered the room, and, without speaking, proceeded to open his pack. "No, thank you, my good fellow," exclaimed Hammerton, "I don't want anything."

The pedlar met this with a deprecatory

shrug of his shoulders, and continued the unpacking of his box. But Hammerton suddenly became conscious of a quick, meaning glance, an impatient knitting of the brows, and a slight but rapid motion of his head in the direction of the waiter.

"That will do, thank you," said the Captain to that latter functionary. "Well, as you've come up I will look at your rubbish, but you must not be disappointed if I don't buy."

"Certainly not," rejoined the Count, in his natural tones, as the door closed. "I am selling, it is true, but not such gew-gaws as these; it's men's lives I deal in."

"The Count!" exclaimed Hammerton. "Deal in men's lives, forsooth! You are juggling with your own when you dare to call upon me at an hotel in Naples."

"I don't see that I run any danger," rejoined Patroceni, quietly. "It isn't that I place the slightest faith upon your honour. But, my friend, my mere apprehension would fill graves on the mountain. I don't suppose you care much about Wheldrake and Glanfield, but you would hardly like to have Sir Jasper's blood upon your head, much less to endanger the lives of the ladies." ·

" You surely don't mean to say—— " exclaimed Hammerton.

" I merely mean that my wolves are hard to hold," interposed the Count. " If you knock the driver off the box you mustn't be surprised if the horses get out of hand. Now, what have you got to tell us ? "

" I should have communicated with you before," replied Hammerton, " but you have perhaps not heard of the murder of that unfortunate Matteo ? "

" Yes ; what about it ? "

" I know no more than does all Naples, that he was brutally slain by some one unknown the other night."

" What do the police think about it ? " inquired Patroceni, sharply.

"How can I tell? You don't suppose I've seen anything of them. You may not believe me, but I've been loyal to my mission and carefully kept out of their way. The money will be ready for you in about a week now. I would have sent you word had I only known how."

"No!" said the Count, sternly. "I know you too well to put faith in you. Fool! do you suppose that I really permitted you to draw lots as to which of you should come to Naples? I did; but took excellent care as to who should be the winner. I told you once before that people who quarreled with me generally came to grief. Let me find any treachery on your part, and though you will think yourself beyond my reach you will find yourself mistaken."

"Count Patroceni," replied Hammerton, hastily. "I tell you I am honestly keeping faith with you. You feel you can insult me with impunity while you hold the lives of those dear to me in the hollow of your hand.

Once let them be free and you will give me the reparation one gentleman usually accords another."

Now this was a very pretty defiance as it stood, but it had a palpable blot in it. The Count's reply was obvious. His lips curled as he said:

"One is under no obligation to go out with cardsharpers."

Hammerton sprang to his feet, and for a moment seemed about to throw himself upon Patroceni. Quick as lightning the Count drew a poignard from his vest.

"Stand back," he said, authoritatively, "unless you would die before your time. Like Wheldrake, I have a presentiment, and that is that you will fall by my hand; at present remember you are an ambassador, and that your person, like that of all ambassadors, is sacred. Bring your negotiations here to a conclusion, and then it will be time enough to talk about reparation; though, even then I should require security that you did not come to the ground attended by a *posse* of gendarmes."

For a moment Hammerton's frame literally shook with passion. Then, recognising how completely he was in this man's power, he gulped down his wrath with a tremendous effort.

" You have come to Naples," he said at last, in tones that still vibrated slightly from anger, " apparently to insult me. You are too strong—I am at your mercy now ; but the time will come ——"

" An excellent burst of melodrama, my friend," interposed Patroceni, contempt-uously. " Exit, upper entrance, right, scowling and muttering. As I told you before, when the time does come I've an idea it will be unfortunate for you. At present I think I have no more to say, except this—I shall send an envoy in to see you this day week, when, I trust, you will be able to bring things to a satisfactory conclusion. Had you and Wheldrake not

interfered with my engagements I should
have been content to receive the ransom
close to Naples. Now you must bring the
money to the camp, and you must bring
it in person. Wheldrake I could have
trusted; rightly or wrongly, I distrust you,
and your own life must be security for my
want of faith in you. The agreed sum
once paid, the whole party shall be con-
ducted in perfect safety to the scene of their
capture. There carriages will be awaiting to convey you to Naples, and one and
all, including yourself, need fear no further
molestation unless you provoke it." And
with these words the Count picked up his
pack and departed.

Hammerton paced the room for some time
after his visitor left him. He ground his
teeth with impotent rage at the indignities
he had been forced to submit to. What
evil star had ever led him to cross this
man's path in life? Everything had gone
wrong with him ever since the encounter

with Patroceni. He did not reflect that it was his own unfair play at the card-table that had placed him in the Count's power, that it was his own rascally scheme to ruin Wheldrake which had led to their all coming abroad, and so fall into the hands of the brigands. That the Count carried too many guns for him Hammerton was now painfully aware. He was in the toils of a very superior scoundrel to himself; in the hands of a man of keen brain and iron nerve. He recognised it was futile to struggle against his antagonist, and, as his wrath quieted down, that the best thing he could do, this matter of the ransom once satisfactorily arranged, was to leave Italy, and devoutly hope that Patroceni might never cross his path again—a man, there was good hope, that might find his "career of industry" cut short before long. Brigand chiefs of his calibre sooner or later fell victims to the prices offered for their apprehension; and, though Patroceni's as-

cendency over his followers was mar-
vellous, and their awe of him apparently
immeasurable, still greed of gold would,
probably, ere long induce one of his followers to betray him. If the annals of
history afford numerous instances of won-
drous fidelity in spite of all temptation,
cases are also rife in which a heavy reward
has not failed to produce the traitor it was
designed to. And then, once again, Hammerton grimly reverted to the incredible
fool he had been to continue his intimacy
with Patroceni. After coming to terms
with him, and disgorging his winnings at
Homburg, he ought to have left without beat of drum. But no. Lured by the
insane idea that in Wheldrake he had
snared a pigeon worth plucking, he lingered
on, and an introduction to English society
had been the price of the Count's silence
about his malpractices at the card-table.

CHAPTER VIII.

A BOLD RESOLUTION.

M. LEROUX stands very much in the position of a very fine whist-player whose game
is considerably too scientific for his part-
ner. The police-agent has most thoroughly
hoodwinked all concerned in the elaborate
game that he is playing. Chisel, Giovanni,
Hammerton, and even Pietro, Giovanni's
confederate, have no suspicion of who he
really is or what end he is aiming at. The
one man of all others that he would fain
keep in ignorance of his proceedings
happens not only to have arrived at a sus-

picion of his connection with the police, but also to have formed a misty idea that Leroux is pursuing a course inimical to his interests. The more Patroceni reflects upon his interview with Hammerton, the more he looks back upon Giovanni's intimacy with that elderly stranger at the " Golden Bush," the more convinced he is that either by design or accident these people are in communication with the police. As regards Hammerton, he had, so far, no evidence to go upon ; but that the elderly gentleman who fraternised with Giovanni was what in his own vernacular is termed a *" mouton "* he had no doubt. What should he do ? He had meant to return to the camp as soon as he had solved the problem of Matteo's murder. He had done nothing towards it as yet, and already saw that it was one of those mysteries not cleared up in a day or two. In the meantime he would walk up to the Villa del Reale and look at the Pavilion. Not probable that he would be allowed to go inside it, not probable that it would afford much information, even if he did so. All traces of the murder had, doubtless, been removed by this, and he would in all likelihood only have the looking at a closed tavern for his pains.

He was right in his conjecture. Still there was a knot of idlers there, gazing at the barred door and closed shutters as if the walls would reveal the secret they held. Amongst these loungers a face suddenly caught the Count's attention. "A man I've seen before," he muttered. "I never forget a face. Where on earth have I seen his? An Englishman, too, evidently, by his dress. A face I've seen more than once; but where? Ah, I have it! It is Signor Wheldrake's servant. He loaded for him that day when we shot those covers by the brook at Wrottsley, the—the—ah, Hangers. Waited, too, every day at dinner. I should like to tell him his master is quite well,"

murmured the Count, with a smile; " but
in the exuberance of his spirits he would
probably go off and tell the police I said so,
which would lead to unpleasant complica-
tions."

The Count shouldered his pack, and was
about to leave the gardens when his attention was suddenly arrested by seeing Chisel
touch his hat respectfully to some one. He
turned round, and saw the valet stroll away
in deep conversation with the same elderly
gentleman who was so intimate with Giovanni.

To a man like Patroceni this was a
revelation. He saw danger, he saw treachery
all around him. He knew nothing about
this old gentleman, had no idea what he
affected to be, what he described himself as,
but had no doubt whatever in his own mind
that he was an agent of the police. And
here he was in close communication with
Giovanni, with Wheldrake's servant, and in
all probability with Hammerton. No; he

would be in no hurry to leave Naples. It was more important that he should sift this treachery to the dregs than return to camp. He saw no great danger in staying in the city for two or three days longer, and keeping a watch over things; he could trust Sarini to keep strict ward over his captives, and, should the authorities lay him by the heels, to threaten dire retaliation if a hair of his head was injured.

The veriest villains have as a rule some staunch friend, and the Count and Sarini had gone through so many stricken fields, times of hardship, and deeds of blood together, that their feeling for each other was strong.

Sarini was perhaps the one man in whom the Count felt he could rely unflinchingly. His old comrade would be apt to become classical, and, after the manner of the ancients, sacrifice some lives to his memory should aught happen to him. Patroceni

kept well away from Herr Stein and Chisel.
He was much too clever to give them an
opportunity of noticing him and had not
the slightest idea of appearing before them
again in his present costume.

With great caution and at considerable
distance he watched the pair for some
time. They sat on one of the benches
overlooking the bay and talked earnestly
together for some few minutes. Then they
rose and left the gardens together, but
had not proceeded far before they parted—
the valet touching his hat with the greatest
respect, while the old gentleman bade him
adieu with kindly condescension.

For a moment the Count was puzzled.
Which was he to follow? It was only
for an instant. "What does it matter,"
he muttered, "where that thick-headed
English servant lives? There is no danger
to fear from him. No, no. That old gentleman with his silver-rimmed spectacles is

far more likely to be the cause of trouble. Quite likely he sees as much over those silver-rimmed glasses as I do through these tinted ones of mine. Spectacles are regarded as an aid to sight. They have another attribute, not quite so generally known—they are pretty nearly as good for *non-sighting* other people. Spectacles, as a matter of disguise, have never yet had due appreciation."

Cautiously and afar did Patroceni follow his quarry; and if the police-agent could have only known that for once in his life he, the tracker of men, was being tracked, he would have experienced a new sensation. Honestly, I think Leroux would really have revelled in the situation; he would have felt like a crack *écarté* player, who finds himself opposed to a foeman worthy of his steel; engaged in a game, if agreed upon, looked on as quite fair according to the laws of the mountain, and also perfectly recognised *testé* Bret Harte on the slopes of

California, namely, "As many cards up
your sleeve as you can contrive without
being found out." At length he saw Herr
Stein turn in at the door of the "Golden
Bush," and then Patroceni, with a low
laugh, made his way to his own quarters
in La Vicaria. This was just one of the
adventures that gave salt to his existence;
it was this that had made him a gamester,
a conspirator, aye, even a brigand. It was
this eternally pitting his head, his intellect,
against other men, that was to him the very
elixir of life. He exulted in this sort of
contest—what matter, it was a game of
heads, and in every sense of the word, too;
his life the stake, and small profit to accrue
from the saving of it! There are, and ever
will be, men of this kind—conspirators from
their youth up, who dream of power and
thrones as in centuries gone by men raved
of the philosopher's stone, or, later on, the
alchemists of the "golden secret."

Did they but know it—and both the

combatants in this game of strategy would have felt deeply interested in the result; the one was staking his professional reputation, the other his life; and both were thorough enthusiasts about all the intricacies of such a contest as they were engaged in. Still the Count had the advantage: he already suspected the police of being on his track, and was bent upon clearing up who that elderly gentleman in silver-rimmed spectacles might be. Leroux, on his side, although quite aware of what a clever adversary he had to combat, had no idea that Patroceni was endeavouring to discover his individuality, or, indeed, that he was taking any other than his habitual precautions against police interference with his pursuits.

The thing that now puzzled the Count was how he was to get speech with this friend of Giovanni's without that worthy's presence. As for fresh disguise that was all easy enough. Agent of the police or no, he felt no doubt but what he could pass before that elderly customer of the "Golden Bush" without his having the slightest conception that he was addressing the dumb pedlar, upon whom he had bestowed a cigarette only a few days before. But the Count knew that Giovanni would recognise him at once by his voice, and he was too thoroughly aware of the awe in which he was held by the lower class of his followers not to know that the bandit would be so startled as to inevitably betray his discovery.

He supposed he must try the tavern again, as he did not know where else as yet he was likely to come across Giovanni's friend. But he felt very little hope of obtaining such an opportunity as he wanted there. He felt pretty sure that Giovanni habitually out-sat his companion. His one chance, he thought, would be to follow this man when he left, and trust to scraping an acquaintance with him casually in the streets. But how? On what pretext? Easy to address him, no doubt, on a dozen excuses, but to involve him in conversation there must be something more than this. At a tavern it would be easy, but in the streets—ah! that was a different matter.

The Count, in his room in La Vicaria, pondered over this a good deal. It had to be done, and, of course, he would do it. He had managed many more difficult things than this; but, at the same time, how it was to be done on this occasion did not exactly occur to him.

Patroceni smoked and smoked, and turned this thing over in his mind. At last he conceived an idea which, for audacity, was quite worthy of his genius. He would turn informer on himself! He, Count Patroceni, would profess to instruct the police how to capture himself. He would cautiously consult this old gentleman about how to put himself in communication with the police, guardedly admitting that he had some information concerning the brigands in the woods above Amalfi that he would be glad to part with for a consideration. If he was right in his conjecture that Giovanni's new friend was an agent of the police he would be pretty sure to tumble into that trap, and in his thirst for further intelligence would unwittingly disclose how much he really knew.

The idea was bold; it was Rob Roy in the Tolbooth, with no Baillie Nicol Jarvie or "Dugald Creature" to fall back upon in case of need.

Now for disguise: that was easy and obvious; he must be attired as one of the peasants of those parts. "Then," thought the Count, with a light laugh, "if I am a little bit soft in the head it will perhaps be all the more effective." Could a bystander have overlooked both hands he might have been very much puzzled to predict whether the Count or the police-agent would eventually be the winner;

but about one thing he would have no doubt, namely, that a very few days now must bring them actively into collision.

Leroux and the Neapolitan police could make nothing out of the murder in the Villa del Reale. Whoever Matteo's assassin had been he had done his work effectually and left not a trace behind him.

That it was the work of one man only they had come to the conclusion, on the evidence of the broken glass picked up on the floor of the parlour. It was clear that these represented the fragments of only two tumblers, and this the police held proof that Matteo had entertained but one guest upon that fatal night. This mattered little to Leroux. Quite possible he might never be able to prove it, but he had no doubt whatever as to whom the real murderer was.

So far, indeed, he thought, it had been rather an advantage to him; it had removed one who seemed inclined to keep a vigilant eye on his intimacy with Giovanni, and it

was absolutely necessary, for carrying out
Leroux's plans, that he should have un-
restricted intimacy with that unprepossess-
ing acquaintance. It was considerably past
midday when Leroux emerged from the
" Golden Bush." IIis sitting with Giovanni
had been somewhat prolonged, for there
had been delicate negociations going on
between him and the bandit. It was
evident to Leroux, from the note that
Giovanni had brought him, that the murder
of Matteo had produced considerable stir
in the camp ; though nothing could be
more guarded than Wheldrake's laconic
reply. After the usual formula that they
were all well, but wearying of their captivity, came the significant line—" We have
seen nothing of our host for two days,
though it is hardly likely the tragedy you
mention has aught to say to his absence."

This to Leroux meant much, as he understood it. It told him that Patroceni had
left the camp. Now was the time for him

to execute his surprise, to play for his
great *coup*, to capture the camp, to carry
back the captives in triumph to Naples,
with the brigands handcuffed two and two
at the wheels of his chariot, and that done
to scour the country for their fugitive chief.
In pursuance of this design he had not
only without much difficulty persuaded
Giovanni to forward another *closed* letter
to Wheldrake, but also to forward another
basket of wine to his confederate Pietro.
About this last there had certainly been
some little argument—Giovanni, in the
openness of his heart and the plenitude of
his feelings, having at first declared that
he was quite capable of dealing with it
himself, and it was only when Herr Stein
had administered a long lecture upon the
necessity and advisability of keeping his
confederate in the brigands' camp in good
humour, supplemented with the threat of
the *déjeuners* being discontinued, that Giovanni promised to yield to his wishes.

Having attained his end, but considerably wearied by his task, with a sigh of relief the police-agent rose, wished Giovanni good day, and took his departure. Ere he had gone far up the street he was accosted by a peasant, who, in a vacant manner, asked him where the police lived.

———————

CHAPTER IX.

" DIAMOND CUT DIAMOND."

LEROUX stopped, and from behind his glasses shot a keen glance at his questioner. Nothing to be read in the rather troubled dark eyes, no longer concealed by spectacles, and the somewhat bewildered face that met his gaze. "And what do you want with the police?" he inquired.

"I'm not used to crowds, and you see I get dazed-like when I get amongst all the houses and people in a big town. My home is in the country, out there afoot of the hills towards Amalfi."

" Dear me ! " thought Leroux ; " a neighbour, perhaps an acquaintance, of my good
friend Giovanni. I shall be on intimate
terms with all the country-side there before
long. " And you want to see the police ? "
he continued, aloud.

" Yes ; it's hard to get a living on the
edge of the mountain, signor ; the corn
won't grow, and then they tell me I'm not
very clever and don't know how to make
the most of our bit of land. And then,
signor, I've had bad luck with the goats
lately ; one or two of them have died, and
the others don't have kids as other people's
do. They tell me they are too old, but
I've no money to buy younger ones with."

" But what on earth, my good man,
have the police got to do with all this ? "

" I don't know ; but they tell me there
has been a great murder committed in the
city here, and that the police are offering
a reward to anybody who can give them
any information about it."

"And you think you can?" said Leroux.

"No; what should I know about it? I was miles away from Naples when it took place; but if the police give money for information of one sort I thought perhaps they would give money for information of another; and life is so hard, signor, and money still harder to come by. Can you tell me why it is that some men grow rich and others grow poor?"

The utter vacuous face of the speaker completely baffled the shrewd police-agent. He peered into his questioner's face over his glasses as if he would read his very soul, but saw nothing but a dreamy, far-away look, as if his questioner was already lost in speculation over the problem he had propounded, and was quite oblivious of the object which had brought him to Naples.

"Now, what information is it you have to dispose of to the police?" inquired Leroux, after a considerable pause.

The peasant's face lit up with a cunning smile as he rejoined—

"If I told you it would be no longer mine to dispose of. You might sell it to the police and forestall me."

"I am going that way," replied Leroux, "and will show you where the bureau is: but you are quite right—keep what you have got to tell to yourself. Only remember this: you will have to give the police some idea of what you wish to dispose of, or else they will probably not think it worth their while to listen to you."

"It will be hard that; for I have walked a long way to try and turn an honest penny. Listen!"—and the speaker dropped his voice almost to a whisper as he said— "It's something about the brigands."

"I don't know, but I think that would very possibly fetch its price," rejoined Leroux.

"What do you think they would give? I could show them where they are, but may be they wouldn't care to meddle with them. There are a good many of them, and they are well armed. It would be more dangerous than hunting a single man."

Once more Leroux shot a keen glance at the speaker. Was there covered sarcasm in his remark, or was it made in all innocence? But not a trace of irony was to be seen on the somewhat meaningless face. Patroceni—for of course he it was—enjoyed a singular faculty of being able to assume (with the assistance of some slight "make-up") a half-witted expression that had done him infinite service before now.

"If you can do that," replied Leroux, "I don't doubt but what you will be well paid for it. Count Patroceni is said to be swift and merciless in his revenge. If he happened to escape you might find yourself in considerable danger."

"Life is so hard, signor," rejoined the

peasant, doggedly. "I 'suppose to get money one must risk something."

Leroux was rather puzzled what to do. To go to the bureau of police with this peasant would be to run the risk of confessing his connection with them. He was anxious to know what this man had to tell. It might amount to a mere nothing; still, he could not afford to neglect any opportunity of obtaining knowledge concerning Patroceni and his followers. For instance, he knew nothing about their exact locality. The woods above Amalfi were extensive, impossible to surround, and it was quite likely that, in scouring the woods in search of their camp, to give them the alarm, and on finally discovering it to find nothing but the smouldering fires as evidence of its late occupation. He was getting letters conveyed to this camp; he was getting wine transmitted to it, but even when everything was ripe for his grand *coup* he was painfully

conscious that he lacked a guide thither.
He had for some time built upon inducing
Giovanni to play that *rôle*. But he had of
late very great misgivings upon that subject.
Giovanni, in his greed for gold and wine,
saw no harm in assisting him to communicate with the camp. But from whatever
motives, whether it was from fear or from
that innate sense of shame which forbids
such men to turn informer, he was evidently
staunch to his comrades. Quite clear that
if he suspected danger to them he would not
only instantly withdraw from this surreptitious post that he was at present conducting,
but further give them due notice that the
authorities were on their track. He admitted having had terrible punishment
dealt out to him by the Count; punishment,
too, that he deemed his offence scarcely
warranted. But Leroux could see that he
was perfectly unswerving in devotion to his
chief, and that no gold would induce him to
play the part of Iscariot. Mechanically

Leroux strolled up in the direction of the
Villa del Reale, where the countryman
followed him, with all the apparent confidence that a lost dog displays when meeting
a friend.

"Ah, signor, this is grand," said the
peasant, as Leroux led the way into the
gardens. "Ah, the sea! It is beautiful.
I seldom see it, but I love it: not but what
I am fond of the woods too, and know them
as I shall never know the blue waters.
Would you believe it, signor, I was never
afloat in my life."

"A happy solution of the difficulty,"
thought Leroux. "I dare not take him to
the bureau. What if I give him an hour in
the Bay? Seated in the stern-sheets of a
boat, while two fellows pull us about, one
can talk. Would you like to go on the
water?" he suddenly exclaimed, aloud.

"Oh, signor," cried the *soi-disant* peasant,
"it is too much, but I should be afraid by
myself. These boatmen laugh at us country-

folks, I am told, and they are apt to be rough with us. No, signor, I dare not trust myself."

"Nonsense, man!" replied Leroux. "I will go with you. We will smoke a cigarette on the water this glorious afternoon. The sun is dipping, and it is just the time to enjoy it. You would have plenty of time to trot up to the police-bureau afterwards. As for his Excellency the Count Patroceni and his friends, they will be doubtless picnicking where you left them. Come."

With many protestations of delight the peasant accepted the invitation, and the two men left the gardens to procure a boat.

Two men pitted against each other like two birds in a cockpit—spurred, too, for the matter of that. Unarmed as they both looked, a revolver lurked in the breast of each of them. A few minutes and they were gliding smoothly and swiftly across the blue waters, heading towards Capri, albeit with no intention of reaching that island.

They were out nominally for a row, but in reality it was a duel between two subtle intellects, each vigorously striving to squeeze the brains of the other. The Count undoubtedly started with odds in his favour. He had a vague idea of his companion's position, and naturally gave him credit for being a shrewd, clever man. Leroux, on the contrary, was quite in the dark about his adversary, and, more unluckily still, was grievously under-rating his brain-power. Keen practised hand as the police-agent was, Patroceni had so far imposed on him that he regarded him as a simple countryman, and if not an imbecile at all events somewhat half-witted.

"You know something of these brigands. I daresay you've seen this Count Patroceni, about whom all men are talking?"

"May be I have, there's more see him than wish to."

"And more wishing to than can get speech with him," rejoined Leroux. "I fancy, if you can bring the police and him together, that you will be handsomely paid for such service."

" What do you think they would give ? " inquired the countryman, with an admirable assumption of that look of low cunning so characteristic of his class when their self-interest is aroused.

" I can't say; the police alone could tell you that. I should like very much to see this famous Count myself."

" You, signor; why, what could you want to see him about ? "

" Curiosity, my man," rejoined Leroux. " He is a man of mark, and since his last exploit of carrying off this English milord the city is ringing with stories about him. It seems he has been famous for years. All men have a passion for seeing celebrities."

" If you will make it worth my while I can take you to him," said the peasant, in a low voice.

" Ah," replied Leroux, laughing, " that

is not quite what I meant. No, no, my friend; I've no wish to go up into your forests above Amalfi for an interview with the most famous robber of modern times. I might find it not so easy to come back again."

"You can't think that the Count would venture into Naples? It might be more difficult for him to get back than for you to return to the mountains. This is glorious, signor. I should like to be rowed about and smoke all the afternoon."

"That would be entirely to neglect your business," rejoined Leroux.

"One cannot be always thinking of business," replied the other. "It is only when one is hungry that one thinks of business."

"A mere animal," thought the police-agent; "would like to bask in the sunshine till moved by hunger to exert itself; with hardly brains to be predatory in its habits, and with just enough low cunning to pick up a living by fraud. Quite willing, apparently, to sell the bit of information he has obtained concerning Patroceni. He may be a very useful tool this, and I must see him again, but it must be next time in my own character;" and then Leroux remarked aloud, "We must be going back now, as I am sorry to say I have no further time to spend on the water," and the police-agent motioned to the rowers to turn back.

"It is too soon; I could stay out here for ever. I was never in a boat before. The ripple of the water against the boat-side reminds me of the rustle of the leaves as the wind sighs through the trees."

"The affairs of this life must be attended to," said Leroux, as they neared the quay. "I have a friend who holds an appointment in the bureau; it is too late to-day, but if you take.this up there to-morrow, and send it in to the police-agent, Leroux, he will tell you all you want to know, and I should think you have a chance of driving a very profitable bargain."

"Ah! so many thanks, signor," said the countryman as they disembarked; "I thank you for your kindness to a poor peasant. I thank you for a charming row. I thank you for having shown me how to dispose of my wares to the best advantage. Heaven's blessing upon you, signor! God will be good to one who is so kind to the poor."

Amidst this shower of protestations, Herr Stein scribbled a few lines on a leaf in his pocket-book, tore it out, and handed it to his companion, and then took his departure.

"Dispose of his wares, the scoundrel!" quoth Leroux as he walked away. "He is taking the thirty pieces of silver, and invoking Heaven's blessings on the head of the purchaser."

CHAPTER X.

A RACE FOR THE HILLS.

PATROCENI lounged on the quay, watching the police-agent till he was out of sight. "There is no doubt about it," he muttered. "I was perfectly right. That man is a myrmidon of the police. At whose instigation are they seeking for my whereabouts? Surely, they will hardly be so mad as to take active measures against me while I hold these prisoners in my hand. It can only be at the promptings of one of these fat-headed islanders themselves. My own countrymen would never make such mis-

takes, much less—and his lip curled at the
thought—with Patroceni.   If I've done
nothing else in all these years, I think I
have taught the authorities to understand
that I am a man of my word, and little
given to flinch from the execution of any
threats that I may utter.   No; pressure of
some kind must have been put upon them,
or they would never proceed in this way.
Matteo is a great loss.   He would have
ferreted out the rights of this for me before
the week was out.   I suppose, though, it is
to be accounted for in only one way; that
triple-dyed scoundrel, to whom, apparently,
in sheer perverseness, these unfortunates
would entrust the arranging of their ransom,
is playing fast and loose with everyone.
What madness possessed Wheldrake to
change places with him?   If there was a
man breathing who knew what a scoundrel
Hammerton was, it should have been he.
If there was one man who ought to have
known the risk of leaving a delicate affair

like this in Hammerton's hands, it was Wheldrake. If there was a man who had suffered bitter wrong from Hammerton, once more it was he. What could have been his object? Why did he take the fate of those he loved out of his own direction, and hand it over to a man like this? Well, it is done. Mr. Wheldrake, in a moment of infatuation, has thought proper to interfere with the conducting of my affairs. He is likely to pay for it with his life. I can only say that his blood, and that of his friends, be upon his own head. I will go back not one iota from what I have said: in the meantime the sooner I am off to the mountains the better. I can do no good here, and if the police try to beat up my lair so much the worse for my prisoners,"

Pleasant reflections these for a good many people could they have known them, but the Count was not given to make *confidants*, and that night he vanished silently from the

city and took his way back to the woods
above Amalfi.

Police-agent Leroux was not a little
puzzled by the non-appearance next morning of his acquaintance of the previous day.
He had made every preparation for his re-
ception, had given orders that he should be
at once admitted to his own room as soon
as the scrap of paper he had given him
should be produced. But that money-
seeking peasant never turned up, and as the
day wore on a doubt stole over Leroux's
mind as to whether that peasant had been
quite so innocent as he seemed to be. True,
he thought a stupid fellow like that might
have fallen into bad hands—might be lying
drugged and half-stripped in some of the
lower parts of the city. All this was very
probable; but for all that Leroux could not
get over an uneasy feeling that for the first
time he had come in contact with a spy of
the famous bandit chief, who had guessed

what he himself was. As he thought over their conversation, while rowing about on the Bay, he was conscious that he had displayed over-eagerness to be in possession of Patroceni's exact whereabouts. But surely that stupid peasant could have had no deeper design than he professed—to wit, to dispose of such information as he possessed about the haunts of the brigands to the best advantage. Doubtful, when tested, whether what he did know was matter of much importance, still, in the rather tortuous game that Leroux was playing, he knew that he could not afford to neglect the slightest chance that presented itself. He bore in mind, too, that he was playing against a very clever and very crafty antagonist, one famous for his stratagems, who had passed his life in one incessant struggle with those in authority. And again, Leroux wished that simple countryman would make his appearance and disburthen himself of what he had to tell. If Patroceni should come to suspect that the Neapolitan police were really taking active measures against him, then Leroux knew from his colleagues in the bureau that it would be in accordance with all the traditions of Italian brigandage to put his captives to death. The police-agent might well feel a little grave over this state of the case. He knew well what a mistake of that kind meant, as far as he was concerned—dismissal from his appoint-ment would probably be supplemented by an indefinite term of years at the galleys— till such period, in all likelihood, as his offending had died out of men's minds— and, as by that his very existence would have probably died out of the memory of the ruling powers, that might possibly be his destiny for life. The more he thought it over the more police-agent Leroux felt confirmed in his opinion that there was no time to lose—that it behoved him to strike quickly.

His scouts should leave Naples that night,

and feel their way leisurely forward towards the woods above Amalfi. That a guide to the brigands' camp would simplify matters was without doubt. But this innocent peasant had not re-appeared, and Giovanni had not as yet been aroused to that sense of his wrongs which would induce him to betray his chief. No; he had arrived at a fair idea of the *locale* in which the bandits were encamped; the exact spot he must trust his scouts to discover. The great thing he had to impress upon them, at first, was caution. Let them not be precipitate; be in no hurry to discover the stronghold of Patroceni and his men, but saunter along leisurely as if they had no definite aim; time enough for them to push on in earnest when they heard that Leroux with the main body was close behind them in support.

Such were the peremptory orders that the police-agent gave to his subordinates. He had thought the whole campaign out as carefully as a Marlborough might have done,

and was conducting it on a miniature scale
with as much energy and ability. He had
sounded the advance, and his *tirailleurs*
were already creeping steadily forward.
Like many another great commander, Leroux
waited for some final information, and that
he trusted to obtain at mid-day from Giovanni at the "Golden Bush." No sooner
had he given up all hope of the re-appear-
ance of that open-hearted countryman, with
his secret information for sale, than he had
promptly issued his orders. All he awaited
now was to hear that the last hamper of
wine had been duly received in the camp.
He could not move too quickly after that.
Patroceni's followers were thirsty souls, and
little likely to keep wine-flasks uncorked.
Let Pietro and his friends only appreciate
this hamper to the extent they had done the
previous ones, and, according to Leroux's
calculations, two-thirds of Patroceni's followers would be *hors de combat. Every
bottle of that wine was drugged, and not a*

man who partook deeply of it was likely to recover his senses for many hours.

It must not be supposed that Leroux's men had not received their orders before this. Some of his advanced scouts were already on the other side of Pompeii, and the main body of gendarmerie had already for some days been stationed at that place, with the avowed object of protecting the road to Amalfi from brigandage. Ostentatious patrolling had constantly taken place for the purpose of throwing dust in Patroceni's eyes. And so far it had succeeded. The Count had no idea that the Neapolitan police really contemplated beating up his quarters. He looked upon this as a mere flourish of trumpets for the benefit of the public; a protest from the Government that they intended to stamp out brigandage with a strong hand; a hint to himself that there must be no more kidnapping of wealthy Englishmen, at all events in the neighbourhood of Naples, for some time.

Shrewd as he was it had never occurred to Patroceni that the presence of all these gendarmes in Pompeii was anything more than demonstration. He had a right to think so. He had much experience of the putting down of brigandage by the Bourbons, and knew that the leader of the party was ever to be bought if the transgressors deemed it worth their while. As a rule it was not; it was something like shirking a master in a big public school. The gendarmerie no more wanted to see the brigands than the master does the transgressing schoolboy.

Leroux discovered Giovanni on his accustomed seat at the "Golden Bush," and speedily ascertained from that worthy that the wine had safely reached its destination.

"The dogs! they are longing for a bout of it. I wish I was with them; but his Excellency is away, and Signor Sarini, who holds command there now, is a stern disciplinarian. Santo Diavolo! there would be much desertion from the band if Signor Sarini were chief!"

"You seem to know these followers of Count Patroceni pretty well," said Leroux, laughing.

"Ha! ha! my little man, we dwellers on the country-side are not scared at people of this sort as you city fellows are."

"No," rejoined Leroux, contemptously, "we are scared at them, and yet I don't suppose there's a man in the city who had been visited with such cruel punishment as you—I mean as you describe—for such a trivial offence, who would not have bided his time, and ere long flown like a wild cat at his adversary's throat."

"It's all very well," growled the bandit, "but you don't know his Excellency."

"No, signor. I am an old man, and am scarce likely to make his acquaintance, but if he had treated me as he treated you—I mean your friend—I don't think the length and breadth of Italy would have kept us apart."

Giovanni said nothing, but gulped down another bumper of wine.

"No," he said at length, doggedly, "I will not turn against his Excellency."

"Signor Giovanni," said Leroux, rising, "I regret that I must leave you; it is possible you will not see me again for two or three days, for business calls me in the direction of Amalfi. Why should I disguise it from you, my friend? I have to play a very subordinate part in the arrangement that has been made for the release of these Englishmen. It is possible I may even see his Excellency Count Patroceni, even speak to this man, at whose frown you tremble. I doubt his impressing me to that extent." And Leroux's lip curled as he shook hands with the brigand.

Giovanni slowly finished his wine while he pondered over Leroux's last remark. For once the police-agent had over-reached himself. He had sought to sting Giovanni into revenging his injuries, but he had gone a little too far when he said that he was going towards Amalfi to meet the Count about that matter of the ransom. It began to dawn upon the bandit's slow intelligence that he had perhaps been indiscreet in talking so freely before a stranger. He recollected what mischief his tongue had led him into that day when he was told to watch the Englishman. Surely, he could have said nothing that could by any possibility bring harm to his comrades. That the Count and his followers were in the hills above Amalfi was no news to any one. He had doggedly refused to take part against him; but, ah! there were those letters. He did not know what might come of them. Fool that he had been to take this Signor Stein's gold; and yet there could hardly be harm in a letter, and the gold was bright red gold, and he loved gold, or rather what gold could give him. Still, he felt uneasy in his mind, and suddenly resolved that he would make his way back to the camp, and, at all events, give notice that the people were coming with the ransom for the prisoners. It still in no wise dawned upon his mind that the affable old gentleman who had entertained him so hospitably almost daily was connected with the police. It was a vague feeling of uneasiness that impelled him to hurry back to the hills and give his comrades warning, though what he was to warn them against was by no means very clear to him.

The bandit rose from his chair, and leaving the "Golden Bush" made his way rapidly back to his lodgings in La Vicaria. His preparations for the journey were soon made, and before the sun dropped he was on his way. Three men, speeding rapidly towards that camp on the plateau, and each in ignorance of the others' movements: Patroceni scouring back to his lair amidst the woods to warn his men to be on the alert, and with ominous thoughts concerning some of those captives in his keeping; police-agent Leroux has the like goal in view, bent on pushing on there with all possible speed and the myrmidons of the law at his back; and there again is thickheaded, drunken, blundering Giovanni, dimly conscious of danger, pressing forward to warn all his comrades of undreamt-of perils.

CHAPTER XI.

TO DIE AT DAYBREAK.

PATROCENI, with his suspicions aroused,
sped back to the camp with eyes and ears
open to every sign of danger. He passed
through Pompeii, noticing the gendarmerie
posted there as he did so. He was prepared
for this. He had been informed that in
consequence of the capture of Sir Jasper
and his party the authorities had established
a post there for the purpose of patrolling
the road to Amalfi.

On his way to Naples he had seen himself
that this was true, but it was by no means
to be deduced by that they had the slightest

intention of taking active measures against himself and his followers. He had had too much experience of the powers that be in Italy (the Italy of the days I am writing of) to feel much disturbed about that. But what caught the Count's quick eye at once as he repassed through the town was the great addition that had been made to the force there since some forty-eight hours before. He felt sure that there were at least three of the police where there had been but one before.

"Something more than a demonstration this!" he muttered to himself; "and yet they surely can't be such fools as to attempt to meddle with me under the present circumstances."

When he left the road and struck across country towards the woods he speedily became conscious of unfamiliar faces. He did not pass many men; but he saw figures in the distance, both right and left of him.

Peasants they were apparently; but Patroceni's quick eye detected that if they were peasants they were at all events peasants that had been through the drill-sergeant's hands. He spoke to one or two of them, and the rather lame replies they gave to his questions convinced him that these men were either police or soldiers in the garb of peasants. Rapidly the Count awoke to the conviction that he was passing through a cordon of skirmishers, who were very slowly feeling their way towards the woods where the camp was pitched. He thought he detected a half-tendency to stop him; only none of those he passed quite liked to take that responsibility upon themselves.

"Betrayed!" muttered the Count to himself, as he pushed rapidly onwards. "That scoundrel Hammerton has doubtless gone to the police, in spite of all his asseverations to the contrary, and this is the result. The miserable fools think they can trap

Patroccni. They arc pushing forward this body of scouts, evidently feeling for our encampment. All that force I saw at Pompeii will—they doubtless arc—being pushed forward as fast as possible to the attack. Captain Hammerton, the lives of your friends wax short. When they have seen the sun rise twice they may say good-bye to this world; and for you," muttered the Count, "let your cowardly carcase be within striking distance for a few more days and you also will have done with things terrestrial, even if my own life pays the penalty. Mistake! yes, a mistake!" he continued, as he breasted the hill. "Well! we are all liable to error." And the Count made this reflection in the same sort of spirit that· a benevolent man might have done regarding ill-judged charitable relief. "Had I followed my natural instincts and simply put an end to Giovanni and also Hammerton,— the one dangerous to me through his drunken stupidity, the other from his utter falsity,—I should have been in no straits now, and the chances are two infinitely better men would have been spared."

Insensible, apparently, to fatigue or want of food, Patroceni tramped on the livelong night. He passed that hut on the mountain where Wheldrake had slept on his way to the plateau, pausing there only for a drink of cold water and to hear what the nominal shepherds had to tell him. They formed the extreme outpost of his camp, and in answer to his inquiries replied that they had noticed no strangers about the country. Sarini's vigilance had apparently not yet been alarmed. Patroceni still continued to push on with all the speed he could muster—a wiry, muscular man, with great powers of endurance, which had been tested many a time and oft in his adventurous life.

To reach the camp as quickly as possible was now his object. He had made up his mind he would sacrifice his prisoners at daybreak the next morning and retreat with a picked body of his followers, carrying Sir Jasper with him. One thing only troubled him: What was he to do with the women? He did not want to slay them. Pitiless as he was there was something repugnant to him in the idea of taking a woman's life, and yet it was impossible to take them with him on such a rapid retreat as he contemplated. As for Wheldrake, he had brought his fate upon himself and indeed doomed Glanfield and Jackson to destruction as well. Yes, Glanfield must die: he regretted it; but it was an exigency that could not be avoided. One prisoner was as much as he could be hampered with. As for Jackson—well, a butler more or less was of no great matter in the world. But the women! What was he to do with the women? Ah! he had it! He would leave them behind him. They would be sure to be discovered in a day or two, and would take no harm for that time.

It was late in the afternoon when Patroceni reached the camp, and, sending one of his men for Sarini, made the best of his way to his own tent. Sarini! that was another thing to be considered; what was he to do with his trusty lieutenant, who, though much better, was still too lame for such a rapid march as he contemplated. He had not to wait long before Sarini presented himself and listened quietly to the news his chief brought.

" I made nothing out of Matteo's murder. People are so utterly at fault they don't even know whom to suspect, but it is as well I went to Naples. We are betrayed, Sarini. The police have got hold of that drunken idiot Giovanni. Signor Hammerton, too, I feel quite sure, is in communication with them besides."

"Giovanni!" exclaimed Sarini; " I did not even know that he was alive; I thought your Excellency *dismissed* him from our ranks for good."

"No; he lives, and could they but persuade him to show them the way to the camp they would probably be upon us this night; as it is I passed through their scouts, who are slowly feeling their way across the hills. They don't know precisely where we are at present."

"Your Excellency will not wait for them, I presume," said Sarini; "and the Signor Hammerton's treachery will entail its usual consequences on his friends."

"The prisoners will die at daybreak, with the exception of Sir Jasper," rejoined the Count, curtly. "We don't shoot women, so I shall leave them behind. The rest of us must be many miles away by to-morrow night. There is only one question: What shall we do with you? Your ancle is hardly strong enough, as yet, to stand such hard work as lies before us."

" No, Eccellenza, I should only break down. I shall take refuge in one of the shepherd's huts about. I am not likely to be interfered with, unless Giovanni points me out."

" No," returned Patroceni, quietly, " he'll not do that. He is betraying us unwittingly; he is very stupid and he will drink. The police have got hold of him, and know that he belongs to us. He does not know it, but he lives under perpetual cross-examination. You will run no risk as far as he is concerned."

" Never mind me, Eccellenza, I can take care of myself; but from what you tell me it is very possible that we shall be attacked before daybreak. Between threats and gold our ill-advised friends from Naples will not find much difficulty about getting a guide to our retreat. We shall have an account to settle with Signor Hammerton that neither you, nor I, Count, are the men to forget. And these others: shall you give them notice of their fate? It will be as well, poor devils, to grant them time to make their peace with God."

"Yes, most men have last words and last messages to leave behind them. God pity those, Sarini, like ourselves, with neither kith nor kin, and whose last words can be no more than a prayer for our country! We have spent our lives in pursuit of the grand idea of an Italian Republic; we have been on the crest of every little storm-wave from our boyhood; we have waded through bloodshed, danger, and what the world calls crime—nay, worse, they would more likely say murder! and all to what end? In the vainest pursuit of a chimera that we seem as far from as when we began. It is too late to change our political creed. We must go on, and levy taxes for our country."

Grandiloquent sentences these, such as

fanatics like the Count and Sarini are wont to use in justifying to themselves their deeds of rapine and bloodshed. Much argument of this sort, is rife, I should think, amongst the leading statesmen in those South American Republics that physically and politically live an existence of earthquakes. As for the Count and Sarini, they were the regenerators of Italy no doubt; but it was a regeneration of which the principal idea was that they should be at the helm of public affairs. No other scheme of Government was quite satisfactory to these patriots.

"Yes," continued Patroceni, after a long pause, "it is only just to give men time when possible to make up their accounts in this world. Fetch Wheldrake and Glanfield here; never mind about the servant, he has lived in terror of his life, I fancy, ever since he has been here. It will be a sin to disturb his last night's slumbers."

Sarini stole noiselessly from the tent, not

the first time by many that he had warned men they were to die at daybreak. And in good truth there had been times in his stormy career in which night after night he had expected a like lullaby ere he laid his head on the pillow. A few minutes, and he returned accompanied by the two victims.

" Gentlemen," said Patroceni, with a courteous bow, " I regret to say that I have unpleasant news to communicate to you. I must in my own defence point out to Signor Wheldrake that it was his own rash interference with my plans which has caused this sad necessity. The police are advancing to your rescue—instigated, I have little doubt, by Captain Hammerton. I warned you, gentlemen, what would infallibly be the result of any such movement on their part. I will be perfectly candid with you. To await an attack here would be madness on my part. I should be so outnumbered that if repulsed at first their ultimate success would be certain, whilst the possibility of a retreat would be lost. To carry so many of you with me as prisoners is impossible. The men must die. The ladies I shall leave behind me. A dull day or so is all the inconvenience they are likely to suffer before assistance comes to them."

"I should be very sorry to interfere with any family arrangements," said Glanfield; "but, if you could make it convenient to leave us behind with the ladies, I think it would be pleasanter for all concerned."

"I knew Hammerton was a scoundrel," exclaimed Wheldrake, "but I would never have believed this of him."

"I shall leave you behind, Mr. Glanfield, but I am afraid you will not much lighten the dulness of the ladies. Brigandage has its obligations, and would be a trade of very little use if it were not respected. Communication with the police is death by the law of the mountain. If that law were not strictly kept the arranging of ransoms would be impossible."

"But," cried Wheldrake, "this money is raised, we know!"

"How?" said Patroceni, briefly, as his dark eyes looked through the speaker.

"You duffer!" muttered Glanfield.

Wheldrake hesitated, looked confused, and eventually said: "We have every reason to believe that arrangement to be satisfactorily concluded."

"Mr. Wheldrake," rejoined the Count, "you are either making a statement for which you have no grounds or you are in communication with Naples. Having invariably found you an upright, honourable man, I have no doubt that my latter theory is the correct one. This makes my situation so much more complicated. Gentlemen, I will wish you good-night now, and regret that necessity will compel me to wish you a permanent adieu at daybreak. Make your peace with Heaven to-night, and believe me

that any last wishes you may express will
be most scrupulously attended to. Once
more, good-night. Conduct these gentlemen to their tents, Sarini." And with a
bow that would have done no discredit to
a throne-room the Count dismissed his unfortunate guests.

CHAPTER XII.

LAST WORDS.

"To die at daybreak." It is not as a rule that, except through the mouth of her Majesty's judges, this sentence is dealt out to us. Regarded theoretically those four words do not carry much weight. The assault will take place at daybreak; if it makes the pulses of the soldier beat quicker it carries no presage of his impending fate. There is promotion, the V.C., and the chance of exceptional honours before him, and in the hot tide of battle who recks that he may be numbered amongst the

slain? But the words "To die at daybreak" assume a very different aspect
when you know there is nothing to interfere between you and implacable fate, and
at sunrise you are to take your last look
upon this earth of ours and sink without
a struggle into the grave which destiny
has awarded you.

A grim prospect this for the few short
hours that remain. No time now to right
that tangled web we most of us make of
our lives. Sins, follies, errors of judgment,
must, such as they are, be left standing
on the record against us. No time left to
us to put right these miserable mistakes
of our career. We are to die at daybreak!
Only a few hours left in which to endeavour
to repair such wrongdoing as may lay heavy
on our soul.

Wheldrake and Glanfield were not
troubled with remorse or compunctions of
this nature. They were both men who had
lived their careless lives honestly and

straightly, according to their lights. If they were to die it was through no fault of their own. To say they could conscientiously show a blameless record would be to claim for them what no men of the world like themselves could possibly produce; but both of them could say with a clear conscience that neither man nor woman was the worse for having known them.

"It looks ugly, old man," said Glanfield, as, upon regaining their tent, he lit a cigar. "Unless something turns up in our favour I fancy that ungrateful beggar really does mean shooting us at daybreak. By Jove! only to think that not a twelvemonth ago, when we shot the Hangers, I could have forestalled him, and rolled him over like a rabbit—by mistake."

"Yes," replied Wheldrake; "there's no jesting about the Count, you may depend upon it. Whether Hammerton has really played false to us or not is of very little consequence. Patroceni thinks he has, and that's enough to determine our fate. Well, it's rather hard. Three or four weeks ago I think I should have rather welcomed the ending; but then, you see, I hadn't again met Maude. I had no idea she still loved me. The world to me was a blank, and I cared not how soon I was quit of it. Now everything is different. I know I still hold her heart. Life once more opens before me, and I am loth to leave it."

"Ah! it's not such a bad sort of place, you know. I've always found it good enough for me. A little depressing, perhaps, when all your fancies at Ascot and Newmarket persistently run second. When the sporting papers on the Saturday clearly demonstrate they ought to have won if such-and-such had taken place, and you only know they didn't, and there's a lot to pay on Monday. There! it's all very well, Cyril; I am trying to take the most gloomy view I can of it, because our places seem booked by this train, and it's no use making faces over it."

"No, Jim," rejoined Wheldrake; "like most Englishmen I suppose we know how to die now our time has come. But there's one thing—I should like to say good-bye to Maude. And, though they mean shooting us at daybreak, I don't suppose our captors will object to that. You, also, I should think, would like to take leave of her."

"Yes, of course," rejoined Glanfield, as he emitted a heavy cloud of smoke from beneath his moustache, "I should like to do that. Don't want to interfere with your good-bye, you know, old fellow. I should like to shake hands too with Mrs. Fullerton. We're old friends, you know. Yes, very old friends; and it would be——" and here Jim took his cigar from his lips, and there seemed something wrong in the rolling of that tobacco which required immediate seeing to. "Yes, old friends," he continued;

"she is a fine woman, Mrs. Fullerton, and a deuced nice woman too; and it would be a polite attention, you know, to say good-bye."

"It is merely asking our gaoler's permission I fancy," said Wheldrake; and, going to the door of the tent, he requested the sentry to pass the word for Sarini. That worthy quickly made his appearance, and upon learning their request acceded to it at once.

"Certainly, signors; I regret as much as his Excellency that the treachery of a friend consigns you to the tomb. The fortune of war, my friends—and something may intervene even now, signors, to save you. I have been half-a-dozen times as near my end as you are apparently, and seen many a year roll by since. Any liberty you like to-night, signors; but remember, attempting to pass the sentries is merely anticipating the morning."

"You need fear nothing of that sort,"

rejoined Wheldrake. " We regard escape as much too hopeless an enterprise to be worth attempting. We only wish to say good-bye to the friends we are so soon to leave behind us."

" I will send word to the ladies," rejoined Sarini, with a low bow. " It is a glorious night, and the plateau will be pleasant. Lives, Signor Wheldrake, must give way to circumstances. But believe me when I say that I am sorry circumstances compel his Excellency to sacrifice yours. Ah," continued this philosopher, " another shake of the dice-box and Patroceni and I will probably change places with you."

" I say," said Glanfield, as Sarini left the tent, " this is all devilish fine, you know ; but if there's one thing that I hate on leaving a country-house it's the saying 'Good-bye.' It's awful awkward, you know. If you say too much about what a good time you've had—looks as if you were fishing for an invitation to be asked there again ; and,

if you take the other line, then I always
picture 'em while I'm on my way to the
station as saying, 'Cantankerous beast!
I suppose there was nothing here good
enough for him.' No, Cyril, you needn't
smile; there's nothing to grin about in
being shot at daybreak, and there is nothing
very jocular in saying good-bye to people
——well, people you care about, for a
precious indefinite period."

"Come along," said Wheldrake, "it's no
use straw-splitting like this. I'm going to
have a last talk with Maude; as for you, I
daresay you will find plenty to say when
you once see the woman who you're head-
over-ears in love with, and who is just as
much in love with you, whenever you can
manage to bring that little explanation
about."

"Mrs. Fullerton in love with me!" exclaimed Glanfield.

"Yes," said Cyril, quietly; "she only
wants to be assured of your love to own it,

but perhaps, standing as we do on the brink of the grave, you have no business to tell it. Come along;" and the two slipped out into the moonlight, where already the flutter of the ladies' dresses was visible.

" I am so pleased to see you, Cyril," said Maude, quietly. "Have you any news from Naples? Papa is getting so fidgety and uneasy. He has taken it into his head that my cousin Fred is playing us false."

" Yes, my dear Maude," rejoined Wheldrake; "and, what is still worse, Patroceni has taken the same idea into his head."

" You don't mean that?" cried the girl, eagerly. "Will it endanger our position here, do you think?"

"I don't know," replied Wheldrake, quietly. "It means that Jim and I have got to leave you for a little."

"Leave us! Good heavens, Cyril, what do you mean?"

"Oh, I don't know. No prudent man puts all his eggs into one basket. I suppose we represent, in some shape, stocks, shares, what you will, to these scoundrels. They don't mean to keep all their prisoners in one place."

"And where are they going to send you?" cried Maude, breathless with excitement.

"Well, I don't know," rejoined Cyril, quietly. "But it will be a good way from here. I shall be saying good-bye to you now for many a long day."

"Long day!" cried the girl excitedly, as she clasped his arm. "What is it you mean, Cyril? Tell me the truth at once."

"Really, Mr. Glanfield, those two are getting a little too lover-like to desire super-vision. I can shut my eyes as close as any chaperone in Europe, but I know when it is time to turn my back—and don't you think, Mr. Glanfield, it is time now?" and with these words the widow turned on her heel and led the way towards the other end of the plateau.

Glanfield walked by her side as they

paced away from the other two still talking in the moonlight.

"What does Mr. Wheldrake mean?" inquired the widow, sharply, the moment
they were out of earshot. "There is surely
nothing serious threatening? You are both
going away. When? why? where?"

"Don't know exactly where," rejoined
Glanfield. "Why—because it suits Count
Patroceni to send us there. When—at daybreak to-morrow morning. Now, Mrs. Fullerton, you know all that I can tell you."

She looked at him for a few minutes and
then replied quietly, "I perhaps know all
you will tell me, but by no means all you
can. There is nothing wrong about the
ransom, is there?"

"Don't suppose so," said Glanfield.
"Hammerton's not written—couldn't perhaps. Post here a little irregular, you see."

A somewhat similar scene was taking
place about twenty paces from them.

"Cyril," said Maude, in a low whisper,

the moment the others were well out of
hearing, "you are not telling me the truth.
What is the meaning of going away—what
is the meaning of our not meeting for ever
so long? Surely you don't think that this
terrible Count can meditate such crimes as
men in his profession too often resort to?
He is not—not—threatening the lives of
you and Mr. Glanfield, is he? Let me see
him, if it is so. He must listen to a woman;
he must know, when it is pointed out to
him, that it will be sheer madness to take
the lives of any of us—that my father will
pay only to save the lives of all of us. And
Cyril, dearest, it might be well he should
know that if he kills you my father need
pay no ransom for me."

"It is no use being frightened, darling.
You have guessed so much that I won't disguise from you that the Count has been
rather lavish of threats this afternoon; and
rather lavish of his wine too apparently," he
continued, as the boisterous laughter of the

brigands, carousing upon the edge of the wood, fell upon their ears. "I'll be honest with you, Maude. Patroceni is anxious, because he thinks your cousin Fred is in communication with the police. We run no danger unless that is the case."

"Oh, Cyril, Cyril! and it was to please me—it was to save my cousin from possible danger—that you changed places with him. Oh! my God. What shall I do?" And the girl threw her hands to her temples. "I, who would give my life's blood for you, am about to become your murderess;" and, snatching his hand, Maude fell at Wheldrake's feet, in a perfect storm of sobs. He raised her in a moment, and, clasping her in his arms, kissed away the tears.

"You have no right to say such things," he exclaimed at last; "the whole thing seems to me to be a puzzle. I have no reason—goodness knows—to think well of Fred Hammerton; but I do not believe him such a scoundrel as this would prove him to be.

The whole thing is a bit of a puzzle; but I fancy it will come out all right in the end. You must not cry for me yet, Maude. Gentry like these, whose hospitality we are enjoying, are wont to get a little fidgety about the bill, more especially when there is some slight delay in paying it. Don't fret, my darling. It is quite possible Glanfield and myself will not be sent away to-morrow morning after all."

The girl looked up into his face in the moonlight, and scanned it eagerly to see if he were keeping aught back from her; but his quiet tranquillity baffled her, and she dropped her eyes after a minute with a quiet assurance that if he and Mr. Glanfield were going away to-morrow morning it was only that they were to be confided to stricter custody.

Mrs. Fullerton had paced up and down for some time by the side of her escort in silence. As for Jim Glanfield he said nothing, deeming it much the safest thing to do, under the circumstances. He was the last man in the world to make any parade of what he would term "an awkward fix" to any lady. If he was to die, well and good; those who were sorry might shed tears for him afterwards, but he was not going to have any drenching of pocket-handkerchiefs in anticipation. He most decidedly had no desire to quit this world, and thought vindictively, could he but have forecast things, that he would have had a *gun accident* that day they shot the Hangers, and cut short the line of the Patrocenis.

"Now, Mr. Glanfield," suddenly exclaimed the widow, abruptly, "you are going away at daybreak. No more fencing, if you please. Where? This monster does not menace murder, does he?"

"Well, you see, these fellows always do; it's part of their business, you know. If the flies that get into their webs don't happen to shell out freely and shortly they threaten them with extinction. All pure bunkum, of course. A man pays as high as he can for his life, but you can't reckon upon his heirs paying a fancy price for his remains."

"Mr. Glanfield, how can you talk in such a dreadful manner?" said the widow, beginning to whimper, and putting her pocket-handkerchief to her eyes. "If—if—you can afford to make a jest of such a thing, you might remember other people have feelings. You might remember that we have likings and dislikings; and bear in mind that when those we love—I mean, like—are in danger, we don't, that is we do, feel very unhappy about it." And here Mrs. Fullerton commenced sobbing in good earnest.

"No; don't do that, you dear little woman, there's nothing to cry about." And here, as Glanfield said afterwards, he never quite understood how it happened, but his arm got round the widow's waist and he found himself kissing away her tears and protesting that he could not afford to give up life at present, as a new interest in it had suddenly dawned upon him.

But the tenderest love-tale must finish at last, and a self-contained man like Glanfield was under no circumstances likely to be very diffusive. It might be questioned whether a man doomed to die at daybreak had any right to speak such words, but men bound for dangerous enterprises have often unburthened their hearts in this wise, much as it might look as if nothing ever come of it. Mrs. Fullerton, having released herself, and finding her lover wax taciturn, began to think it was time to retire and exult over her conquest.

"I shall feel dreadfully uneasy," she said, "till I know this money is paid. I think it can only mean that Count Patroceni is determined to put on still further pressure. It will be an anxious time for all of us until the next few days are over.

Meanwhile, Maude and I must retire. Sir Jasper betook himself to rest an hour ago."

Maude turned at her aunt's summons, and the two men escorted the ladies to the door of the hut. It was no time for conventional partings, but Mrs. Fullerton was just a little surprised when Wheldrake kissed her as he bade her farewell.

———————

CHAPTER XIII.

HOW SOUND ARE THEIR SLUMBERS.

FORTY-EIGHT hours after Hammerton's interview with the Count he received a visit from Chisel. The valet had occasionally called before to know if there was any news of his master, and, upon this occasion, he sent up not only his name but a note to say that his business was urgent. Hammerton ordered him to be shown up, and Chisel said at once :—

" I am afraid, Captain Hammerton, there is mischief brewing. You know, sir, before you arrived in Naples I had been urging the police to search for my master; but

after you told me that I was endangering
his life by so doing I never went near them.
Well, sir, there was one of the subordinates
there, who spoke a few words of English,
who used to be very civil to me, and he
promised to let me know when they heard
of anything. He came down this morning
to see me, and told me I should soon see my
master now, as the police had sent a great
expedition, headed by about the cleverest
man amongst them, to capture Patroceni
and all his band; and when I hinted that
Count Patroceni, by all accounts, was a
hardish nut to crack, he told me their men
were in such force as to make any resistance
on the part of the brigands hopeless."

"The fools! the madmen!" exclaimed
Hammerton; " the brigands are much too
alert, and know the country much too well,
to be surprised by the gendarmerie. The
sole result of their interference will be the
murder of the prisoners. There is only one
thing for it; I must get a hack, and make

my way thither as quickly as possible," and
Hammerton at once rang the bell and gave
the necessary order to the attendant.

"Pleasant this," he thought. "If I do
not get there before the police I shall
naturally be regarded both by Patroceni
and his prisoners as their betrayer. I
played Wheldrake a pretty scurvy trick
that night at Wrottsley, but then he stood
between me and thirty thousand pounds.
Since then he has risked his life for mine;
and I can't let him nor the others die with
the belief that their blood is on my head.
No; if horseflesh and my legs can do it I
must be on that plateau before the police."

In vain did Chisel beg for leave to accompany him. Hammerton curtly refused that
request. "No," he said; "one man will
attract less attention. I will go alone; but
remember if I should not return you will
bear witness that I never went near the
police, but did my very best to prevent the
catastrophe of their coming."

Another minute and Hammerton was in the saddle, and speeding as fast as his horse could carry him upon the road to Pompeii. As he passed through it he noticed that there were no gendarmes about, and he had heard at Naples for some days past there had been a strong post of them there, for the purpose of patrolling the road to Amalfi. Yes; he had no doubt that Chisel's information was true, and that all these men were now moving up to surprise Patroceni's camp. He continued to push on as quickly as possible, showing very little mercy to the horse he was riding. He had diverged now from the high road, and was making his way across the hills towards the dark woods he could see in the distance. At last he reached the shepherd's hut, where Wheldrake had slept with his captors on his way to the camp. There he was confronted by Giovanni. The bandit had paused for a short rest, and was engaged in conversation with two or three comrades who were there, as a sort of outlying picket. They were listening intently to the news that Giovanni brought. No sooner did the bandit catch sight of Hammerton than he arose and advanced towards him in a threatening manner; but the Captain throwing up his hands in sign of amity, and being moreover quite unarmed, the ruffian withdrew his hand from his poignard. In his broken Italian Hammerton succeeded in making Giovanni understand that he had urgent business with the Count, and then again one of the *soi-disant* shepherds recognised the Captain as having lately been one of his Excellency's visitors; so, taking into consideration that he was unarmed and alone, Giovanni thought there would be no harm in acceding to Hammerton's request that he should accompany him to the camp. That bandit was soon ready to start again, and they pushed forward on what was the more intricate part of their journey.

It soon became evident that the English-

man was far the fresher of the two men.
In the first place he had led a far healthier
life of late than Giovanni; and in the second
place the bandit was weighted besides with
the effects of the serious illness that had
followed upon the results of Patroconi's
rough treatment. Then again Hammerton
had come all the first part of his journey
on horseback, not having abandoned his
cruelly-gruelled hack till reaching that hut.
Those elaborate luncheons at the " Golden
Bush " began to tell their tale on the hill-
side, and the brawny bandit drew his breath
with many a sob. Hammerton cast impatient glances at his companion and urged
upon him the necessity of greater speed.

" It is of no use ! " gasped the bandit.
" I can go no quicker. I am pretty near
finished as it is."

" But the case is urgent," rejoined Hammerton. " The police are on our heels, and
the Count and your comrades must have
warning."

" Push on by yourself, then!" cried the panting Giovanni. "I tell you again I can go no quicker and am nearly worn out. Surely the road is clear enough to you now."

" Point it out," answered Hammerton, briefly.

" You see that stunted tree to the right," rejoined Giovanni, stopping and throwing himself on the ground; "keep just inside that. You can see the edge of the woods already. When you are past the tree keep as straight for them as you can, bearing if anything a trifle to the right. When you near them look for a big boulder. There are several smaller scattered about, all of the same size; but you must look for one double the size of its fellows. Just behind that you will find a narrow path through the woods. You can hardly mistake your way, and when you come to the spring turn to your left, and in a couple of hundred yards or so you will hit the brook;

follow that upwards and it will lead you into the camp."

All this took some little time to explain, and when Hammerton was about to start again Giovanni sprang to his feet and protested that he would go with him, but it was an expiring effort. Before he had proceeded a quarter of a mile his endeavours to keep pace with his companion had completely exhausted him. He once more threw himself on the ground and cried, "Go on, never mind me. One caution only—answer pretty quickly when challenged, for our people are apt to be pretty handy with their guns to night visitors."

Hammerton pushed steadily forward until he came to the boulders. It took him some few minutes to find the king-stone. That found he speedily discovered the path Giovanni had described, and pursued it at his best pace till he came to the spring. By this time it had grown so dark that he

was afraid to leave it, and sat himself down
by its side till the moon should have risen
a little higher in the heavens. According
to his directions he should now leave the
path and penetrate through some two
hundred yards of wood until he hit the
stream.   But without a little more light
it was very easy to get turned round and
lose all knowledge of the compass in that
short distance, so he wisely determined to
remain where he was.

Fatigued with his exertion, he stretched
himself by the spring, and in a few minutes
fell asleep.   About the time that Wheldrake
and Glanfield were bidding a last good-bye
to the women they loved on the plateau,
and walking back to their tent to make their
grim final preparations, incumbent as a rule
on men doomed to die at daybreak, Hammerton stretched himself and awoke.   The
moon shone gorgeously by this, and he had
now little difficulty in striking the brook.
In accordance with his directions he followed

it upwards, but had not gone twenty paces before he became aware of a man leaning his back against a tree, and apparently buried in profound slumber. His gun lay on the ground by his side, and his arms hung loose and nerveless across his body. He advanced cautiously towards him, but the man showed no signs of awaking, and speedily he jumped to the conclusion that this was one of the cordon of sentries, whom slumber had overtaken. What should he do? To pass him might be dangerous. To awake him were more so. There is a proverb about "letting sleeping dogs lie," but Hammerton thought his presence within the sentries, unless duly announced, might be more perilous. He decided to awake him. Getting between the man and his gun, he put his hand quietly on his shoulder. He slept on unconsciously. He shook him, but still, so sound was his slumber, without effect. Suddenly a thought flashed across him. Could he be dead? He tore open his jacket, placed his hand to his heart, and his ear to his mouth. No, the heart beat steadily, if feebly, and the breath came regular, if low. It was like the discovery of one of the seven sleepers. Slowly following the stream, in about another hundred yards Hammerton came to another brigand in like case with his comrade. He shook him similarly, but with no effect. What could it all mean? A little further, and he came to the stones that crossed the brooklet. He passed to the other side, and found himself in the midst of a group of a dozen or fourteen bandits buried in slumber so profound that not one of them moved a finger at his presence amongst them. He made his way quietly to the plateau, and, pausing for a moment under the shadow of the wood, considered what he had better do. He knew these men were fond of wine, but it was impossible they could all be so utterly overcome as this by any ordinary drinking-bout. The best thing he could do, he thought, was to go boldly across the plateau straight to Patroceni's tent. He moved. Just as he was about to step forward a footstep on the turf, at his side, made him start, and, before he could well distinguish the new comer, a strong hand gripped him by the throat, and he felt the cold barrel of a pistol pressed against his temples.

———————

CHPTER XIV.

DEATH OF GIOVANNI.

"You had better go quietly, signor, for I am in little mood to be trifled with. Make the slightest resistance and you will die."

"I have no intention of making any resistance," replied Hammerton, quietly comprehending Sarini's speech, more by his action than his words.

"You will come, then, to his Excellency;" and Sarini, assured that his prisoner meant no resistance, released his grip, with the comforting assurance that he would shoot him at the slightest sign of any endeavour to escape.

They traversed the plateau rapidly, and in a few moments stopped at the door of Patroceni's tent. Still keeping a vigilant eye on his prisoner, Sarini sharply called :

"Your Excellency! Your Excellency!"

The Count was a light sleeper, and in a moment he appeared at the door, already dressed.

"What is it?" he demanded.

"We knew that we were betrayed; but the enemies are rather closer to us than we thought. Our fellows are all drunk. I have just been round the camp for the second time to-night, and there is no rousing them. I can't understand it. They were drinking when I went my rounds the first time; and I cautioned them that there were hawks abroad, and they were to have a care not to drink too deeply. Two or three of them might have forgotten the caution; but I cannot understand their all being in such a state of utter insensibility."

"Captain Hammerton," said the Count,

sharply; "you've been rash to venture once more into the tiger's den. We agreed once before that you would not stick at trifles to lay your hand upon thirty thousand pounds. It is a bold game; but it's like to be a fatal one to you. Well thought out; well thought out! Win your cousin's hand or not, Sir Jasper was bound to do something pretty liberal for the man who dared so much to save him thirty thousand pounds."

"You mistake me altogether, Count. I have risked my life, I know. Risked it not to keep faith with you, but for the sake of those whose lives you hold in your hand."

"Thanks for your information," sneered the Count. "I discovered that for myself when I had the pleasure of seeing you in Naples. Even conversed with the police spy, who is fool enough to think that he has circumvented Patroceni. Come to warn me, forsooth! You have come with the police at your heels. Hold, Sarini! I will go round for myself. You will take care of our enterprising friend here. If he moves a finger you will know what to do," and the Count rapidly crossed the plateau. He came first to the sleeping group, opposite the stepping-stones of the brook. He looked around at the scene of the revel—half empty wine-flasks, tin pannikins in which the liquor still stood.

Patroceni shook two of the sleepers. "As I thought," he muttered. Then, stooping down, he raised one of the half-filled pannikins to his lips and tasted it. Again he rinsed his mouth with the contents, then spat it cautiously out on the grass.

"*Drugged!* And pretty stiffly too. A clever plant. That agent of police who planned this *coup* is rather cleverer than I gave him credit for. How did he get his wine into the camp?" And pondering over that problem the Count crossed the stream, and proceeded further down the opposite bank. He came one after the other to the

sentries that Hammerton had passed, and
striking across to the spring followed the
track towards the boulders some little
distance. He listened attentively for quite
ten minutes, but no sound reached his ear,
save the faint rustling of the trees.

Then Patroceni turned back, and rapidly
went round amongst his men; he found
them all more or less senseless. Some of
them indeed, when shaken, awoke for two or
three minutes, and made some attempt to
rise; but the fatal lethargy soon overtook
them again, and they sank back to resume
their disturbed slumbers. Some there were
who were no more to be roused from their
insensibility than so many corpses. A
frightful imprecation escaped Patroceni's
lips as he recognised the crafty treachery
that had been practised on him, and he
made his way back to his tent in a frame
of mind that boded small mercy for his
prisoners.

He entered the tent where Sarini, pistol

in hand, was keeping grim watch upon his captive.

"It is as you said," he exclaimed; "treachery foul and ingenious has been practised on us. Captain Hammerton, if you would make your peace with the Church you had best do it to-night. You will die with your comrades at daybreak."

"I have been fool enough," rejoined Hammerton, "to do my best to warn you of the approach of the police. I suppose I shall pay the penalty for having tried to behave honestly to you for once. There is one thing, Count, make no mistake about it, whatever blood you shed here is likely to be speedily avenged. I know the state of your followers, and once more warn you, as I did before, that the police will be upon you before many hours have passed. Fly! leave us, and trust to me that the money shall be paid, wherever you choose to name."

"Trust to you!" interposed Patroceni, scornfully; "it would argue much want of intelligence if I did. No. Your plan was ingenious, but Sarini and myself are old conspirators. I do not intend you should live to enjoy the profits of your treachery. There will be little fear," he continued with a sneer, " of your imitating Iscariot *now*. The ending of *his* history is just the part you would omit; " and as he finished the Count made a sign to his lieutenant, who promptly pinioned Hammerton's arms from behind.

" Don't struggle," said Patroceni; " we are two armed and determined men, and, of course, can kill you now if we wish to. It is better to wait a few hours, and see whether luck may not turn in your favour. In the meantime, when the prisoners outnumber the garrison, it is only common prudence to bind them." And in another minute or two Hammerton found his arms pinioned behind his back. That done, the Count pointed to his bed, and bade him take the rest he must require. Tired and worn out as he was, in spite of the discomfiture of his bonds, Hammerton was soon asleep.

Giovanni, in the meanwhile, after a short nap, in some measure recovered from his fatigue, pushed rapidly forward, passed the boulders, followed the track up to the fountain, struck off through the wood, and, as Hammerton had done some two hours before him, came to the first sentry on the brook. Like Hammerton, he was astounded at the stupor in which he found him, and his amazement was still further increased by discovering the next in pretty much the same state. But when he had crossed the brook his astonishment knew no bounds. He gazed critically at the relics of the revel, and a fear came over him as the insensible forms of his comrades met his eye. Giovanni could certainly claim to be a judge of drunkenness in all its phases; but, as he shook first one and then another of his fellows, and failed to rouse them from their heavy trance, a feeling of terror came

over him. "This is not drunkenness," he
muttered, turning white almost to his lips,
and kneeling down by the prostrate form of
his old friend Pietro. "Santa Diavolo! they
are poisoned!" Once more he looked around,
and a wine-flask at Pietro's side met his
eye. He raised it, and, under any other
circumstances, would, probably, have swallowed the remainder of its contents; as it
was, he gazed at it curiously, and promptly
recognised that it was one of that pattern of
which the Signor Stein had been so lavish.
He understood it now. Pietro had invited
his comrades to have a bout over the last
basket that he, Giovanni, had forwarded.
Merciful heavens! that wine must have
been poisoned. That villainous old man
had dealt with his brethren as if they were
rats.

He sank on his knees in the extremity of
his terror. This man—whose life had been
stained with crime, who had only recently
committed a double murder—now cowered

in unutterable horror at the thought of
having been, though unwittingly, the destroyer of all his companions.

"They were good to me, some of them,"
he muttered. "If it had not been for Pietro
and two or three more I should not be alive
to poison men like rats. I have slain more
than one in my time, but it was by bullet or
steel. I never sent one to his grave in such
cowardly fashion as this. Holy Virgin, the
place will haunt me. I shall see it in my
dreams, and their ghosts will point and
gibber at me from the brookside here. I,
who have broke bread and drank with them,
to poison their wine-cup!" and the terrified
man literally grovelled on the ground at the
idea of the death-plague he had scattered
round him. "Are they all dead?" he murmured. "Surely his Excellency did not
touch it. And Signor Sarini? He must be
alive. What am I to do? I dare not go
forward, the way seems strewn with corpses;
as if Matteo and that miserable woman were

not enough to see in the night-time. He died hard, did Matteo; but it served him right. No fault of his he did not cause my death. I did his, and, coward as he was, how he fought! But I was mad with drink that night, and my eyes red with blood. I'd have killed him had he been twice as strong. And that fool of a woman; what impelled her to come upon the tiger just as he had struck down his quarry? Well, she died too!"

He uttered the last words half unconsciously aloud. A mocking voice promptly answered him.

"Don't fret yourself on that point, Giovanni. You are about to follow them." And himself on his knees, the bandit saw his chief standing a few paces from him, with his pistol levelled at his head. "This, you scoundrel, is, I presume, your work. I saw you myself at Naples in close conversation with the police. It is through your means they have introduced this half-

poisoned stuff into the camp, whereby you
consign the whole of your comrades to
the grave or the galleys. It was foolish
of me to give you such a slight chance
for your life as I gave you last time. I
might have known if you lived I should
repent it. Don't think I am going to make
that mistake again."

"You saw me in Naples, Excellency?"
stammered Giovanni.

"Yes. You've not forgotten the 'Golden
Bush,' I should think. Perhaps you remember the dumb pedlar, who sat at the
next table to you at luncheon. I was that
pedlar, and the man you were lunching
with was a police-agent. Quick! Your
time is short. Was it not you sent this
wine?"

"Yes, your Excellency; but I knew not
that it was anything but good wine."

Giovanni was much less terrified at the
wrath of his chief than at the phantoms
his imagination had conjured up just before.

"And that pleasant old gentleman with the spectacles gave it you to send, I suppose?"

"*Si, Eccellenza*," replied Giovanni.

"Then go as herald to those whom your drunken stupidity has doomed to destruction;" and as he finished the Count's revolver cracked, sharp and shrill; and Giovanni had preceded his comrades across the Styx. "There will be no resurrection this time." The Count's bullet had sped straight and true, and Giovanni fell back, shot through the heart.

CHAPTER XV.

LEROUX ARRIVES AT THE PLATEAU.

As Giovanni rolled over a veritable corpse among so many apparent ones, Leroux with his men had reached the edge of the woods. There he halted his main body while with his scouts he sought for the path, of whose existence he was now aware. From one or two frightened peasants whom he had made prisoners on the way he had extracted a very fair idea of the road to Patroceni's retreat. He had made no mistake so far, but it was just this last bit through the woods that was difficult to follow without a guide. There was a delay of some time before the scouts discovered it, and the moonlight was waning when he finally plunged amid the trees.

The most dangerous part of his enterprise had now commenced ; the narrow path only permitted of their proceeding two abreast. The dark hour before the morn was approaching, and they were liable to be attacked by invisible foes at almost any moment. Leroux fancied he had heard a shot when they first came up to the woods, but it was so faint and far away that he could not be sure. The report of a revolver does not echo very far. Slowly and cautiously they made their way along—finger on trigger, and with eyes peering into the darkness. Leroux led the way in person. The wine might or might not have done its work. Such a wary old fox as Patroceni might have discovered this hamper coming into his camp, and would be certain to examine it. At last they arrived at the

fountain. There the path apparently ended,
as the police-agent had been correctly
informed it would. Leroux knew now that
he was very near the brigands' camp, and
that the greatest caution and complete
silence were absolutely necessary. It had
now become so very dark that Leroux
determined to wait for daybreak. He was
quite tactician enough to know that he
could not utilise his superiority in numbers
except in the open. A very inferior force,
knowing the ground and attacking him
here amongst the trees, would be quite on
an equality with him. He calculated that
the first streaks of grey would appear in
the sky in half-an-hour. As soon as it was
fairly light—that is, in about an hour—he
would feel his way to the brook, collect his
men on the edge of it, and then make a
bold rush at the plateau. If the drugged
wine had been partaken of the work would
be easy, but it was hardly likely that so
noted a bandit as Patroceni would be taken

without some bloodshed. It could hardly be hoped that he, as well as all his men, would have fallen into the insidious trap that had been laid for them. Having enjoined the strictest silence on all his followers, Leroux sat quietly down by the fountain to wait for the light.

Leaving the police-agent and his men bivouacking by the fountain, we must now look back upon what is happening in the camp.

After the death of Giovanni the Count and Sarini walked quietly back to the former's tent.

"We must leave this at daybreak," he said; "it's the cleverest snare that ever was set for me. I shall make an example before I go. The police must be made to understand that brigandage is a profession not to be rashly meddled with. There are too many political exiles dependent upon it for a living."

"Are all the men to die, Excellency?"

"No, I think not. We will give Sir Jasper and his old fool of a butler their lives. They will be some consolation to the women until the police come up. They will be here most likely as the day wears on. Of the two men who have betrayed us one has died, the other expiates his treachery at sunrise. The Signors Glanfield and Wheldrake, I regret it, but they must suffer as examples in accordance with the law of the mountains. But, Sarini, we must not forget that there are only our two selves now to administer justice. Don't think me a stickler for etiquette, my old comrade, but you know in the ordinary way we should have paraded the three culprits in a row, bandaged their eyes, unless they professed to be able to look into the levelled carbines without blenching, and shot them in orthodox fashion. As it is we must first of all dispose of Hammerton, and we must deal with the other two in less military fashion. Even when unarmed I have seen men think it worth while to make a throw for their lives, and that there are only two of us might encourage these perverse Englishmen to attempt such folly."

"It will make very little difference, Excellency. It may give a little more trouble; and if you and I can't deal as we list with a couple of unarmed men then the training of years goes for nought. Our nerves are little likely to fail us at the sight of some slight difficulty."

"True; and now off with you! We've time to spare yet, and I've some few preparations to make here before we start." Could Patroceni have heard the conversation carried on in an undertone in the adjoining tent he might have been confirmed in his opinion that these perverse Englishmen were likely to give trouble. Glanfield had been roused from a fitful slumber by the report of Patroceni's pistol. He at once shook his companion.

"Did you hear that?" he said. "It was

a shot close to the camp. Of course, it may
mean anything. It may mean that one of
our drunken captors has discharged his gun
by accident; it may mean that one of their
sentries has mistaken a bush for a police-
officer; it might be that most dangerous of
all things—soldiers advancing to release us.
It is not likely; but there may be a turn-up
in our favour before to-morrow. We are not
struck out of all engagements yet."

"Not quite yet, Jim," replied Wheldrake,
with a faint smile. "Such a very few
weeks back and I would have cared so
little if it were so; but it seems hard now.
Life looks so rosy before one. I am assured
of Maude's love. I have only, on my return
to England, to find Hammerton's confederate to clear my good name. That
should be easy. Yes, life is sweet to me!
it is bitter to die now."

Glanfield put his glass in his eye, and
leisurely surveyed his companion for a
moment.

"Shake hands, old fellow!" he said. "Those are about my feelings, only I should have expressed it as a deuce of a sell. I'll tell you what, Cyril, I don't see why we shouldn't strike a blow for our lives, if we see a chance."

"We are more morally fettered, Jim, than if we were bound hand and foot. The slightest attempt of that kind might cost the lives of those very dear to us. A more ruthless tiger than Patroceni, in spite of all his purring, never existed. Let his prey escape him, and he will rend all within his reach. No, it's hard; but we must die quietly."

"Don't be afraid but what I'll die quietly enough if it comes to that," replied Glanfield, doggedly; "but if I see a twenty-to-one chance for our lives I mean to take it. Even Patroceni would never be tiger enough to harm our sweethearts; and don't you think they would bid us strike a blow to save ourselves if we got a fair chance?"

" You have no business to endanger their safety," replied Wheldrake, sternly.

" There is no use quarreling over it," replied Glanfield. "I am not going to do anything rash; and it is long odds against my getting a chance to do anything at all. But, remember, if I do holloa to you, you can stand out of it, or not, as you like ; but you will see a fight."

Wheldrake made no reply, but threw himself moodily on the bed.

The faintest streak of dawn could be first seen in the sky from the plateau, invisible to Leroux and his men amongst the woods. But the police-agent had become restless, and whispered to the captain of the gendarmerie acting under his orders to remain where he was whilst he crept a little way forward to explore. He took two or three of his own men with him, and then carefully taking his bearings started in the direction of the brook. At an interval of about fifty paces he dropped a man to

ensure his being able to find his way back,
with instructions to reply immediately to a
low whistle. He was surprisingly fortunate;
for by the time he had dropped his last
man he had hit off the brook. Cautiously
he crept along its bank until he came to
that first insensible sentry.

Leroux's pulses tingled. The man seemed
sound asleep;—how sound? Could this be
the first of his victims? Drawing a poignard
from his breast he advanced stealthily to
the sleeper's side. He slept soundly, but
he must know how soundly.

Gripping his dagger close he placed his
hand upon his shoulder. It was well for
that sleeper he had drank deeply of the
cup. Had he suddenly displayed active
animation Leroux's poignard would have
been buried in his breast. But no; he was
senseless as the tree against which he
leaned. Leroux shook him roughly, and
still he moved not. Then the police-agent

uttered a low laugh and, turning on his heel, wended his way quietly back to his men. Leaving the scouts he had placed where they were, no sooner did Leroux reach the fountain than, placing himself at the head of his party, he gave the word to move on, and rapidly led them to the banks of the stream, cautiously preceding them a few yards. Quietly they crept along the bank, the police-agent as he passed the insensible sentry signing to his men to bind him. When they came to the second Leroux's heart beat high. No doubt now that his stratagem had succeeded ! Quietly he made his way till he came to the stepping-stones; then he crossed, It was daybreak on the plateau, and as he cleared the brook which ran along the extreme edge of the wood he came across the scene of that fatal revel, fatal in appearance as that of the famous banquet of the veiled Prophet of Khorassan. Leroux held up his hand as a signal for those behind him to halt, and then stepped forward to investigate affairs.

From where the brigands had held what was destined to be the final drinking-bout for most of them the ground ran with a gentle slope up to the edge of the plateau, so that a man could move about without seeing anything that was going on just above him, nor be seen from that little bit of table-land unless by some one on its edge. The wily police-agent took in the whole scene at a glance. The half-finished wine-flasks, the half-emptied pannikins, the drunken revellers strewn around, looking as if dead. "All this," muttered Leroux to himself, "the simple result of a well-administered opiate. Ah!" he said, with a low laugh, "quite a new departure in the profession—the calling in of medical science to aid in the apprehension of criminals." But suddenly Giovanni's form caught his eye. "That one is not drugged,"

he muttered; "he's dead in good earnest."
In a moment he was by his side, and turned
up his face. "*Mon Dieu!*" he murmured,
as the first fresh rays of the sun fell on the
upturned features of the dead bandit, "my
valued friend with the irrepressible thirst!"
Quick as thought he drew back the dead
man's eyelid; but the fierce light of the
savage orbs was quenched. A slight welling
of blood from Giovanni's chest showed how
he had come by his end. "Shot for his
treachery, no doubt," mused Leroux, as he
stepped quietly back to his party.

His orders were now prompt and decisive.
Rapidly and noiselessly they crossed the
stream, and spread themselves out under
the crest of the slope, with strict orders to
advance with a rush the minute Leroux
gave the signal; then the police-agent crept
cautiously forward, raised his head above
the crest, and saw a sight that for the
moment enchained him.

Standing bareheaded, with his arms pinioned behind his back, was Hammerton; and Leroux's astonishment at seeing here a man whom he believed to be in Naples was unbounded. Six paces in front of Hammerton, pistol in hand, stood the peasant whom he had taken out boating, while a second peasant was anxiously listening to what the first was saying.

———————————

CHAPTER XVI.

THE LAST TRICK IS TURNED.

FOR an instant the police-agent was puzzled what to do. He was nearly a hundred yards away from the impending tragedy. To charge now would be to precipitate it, and yet there could be no doubt as to what Hammerton's doom would be unless intervention arrived speedily from some quarter. He was about to spring to his feet and call upon his men to follow him when his attention was arrested by seeing a man look cautiously from out of one of the two tents which lay on the further side of the three men.

The new comer on the scene evidently grasped the situation at a glance. He bounded out of the tent, and, with a shout which fell clear enough upon Leroux's ears, of "Come on, Cyril, I am not going to stand by and see cold-blooded murder done!" dashed across towards the group. He was much nearer to Patroceni and his victim than Leroux, and in his cricketing days there had been very few quicker men between wickets than Jim Glanfield. Patroceni knew at the first shout that the "perverse Englishmen" were refusing to meet their sentence quietly, but he never turned his head, and, raising his pistol steadily, shot Hammerton through the heart. Sarini on his part turned promptly at the sound of Glanfield's voice, and, upon seeing that his foe was close upon him with the light of battle in his eyes, fired quickly, perhaps a little too quickly, for it is certain that he missed his man; and, as he raised his pistol to fire a second shot, he was confused by

seeing Wheldrake close upon his friend's
heels. He hesitated for a second — fatal
hesitation! for, as his finger pressed the
trigger, Glanfield struck up his arm and
threw himself upon him. As for Patroceni,
having disposed of Hammerton, he wheeled
quickly round, impassible as ever. His
pistol again rang sharp and true: a stumble,
a flounder or two to recover himself, and
then Wheldrake fell forward on his face. A
grim smile of triumph lit up the Count's
features, destined to be short-lived; for, as
he hurried forward to Sarini's assistance,
now engaged in a grapple of life and death
with Glanfield, Leroux's voice rang through
the air, calling upon his men to follow him,
and that they did so closely probably saved
the police-agent's life.

"He has his poignard, and can take care
of the Englishman by himself," muttered
the Count, as he turned to confront this
new danger. At a glance he saw that the
police were upon him. About a dozen

armed men were running towards him in a cluster as fast as they could. Patroceni's eyes sparkled; for one second he stood irresolute, and the next instant his pistol was again discharged, and one of his assailants bit the grass.

But which was their leader? That unluckily was the thing Patroceni could not determine. Three times more did his revolver crack, and twice with fatal results. The ardour of the attacking party perceptibly cooled. With one exception they all halted; but Leroux came on with all the determination of a cheetah.

"Oh, for one more barrel!" exclaimed the Count, as he dashed his now useless pistol at the police-agent's head, and, drawing his poignard, prepared himself for the struggle. "I'll send one more fool to the other world anyhow before I'm their prisoner." In another moment Leroux had sprung at his throat like a wild cat.

They were well matched, and Leroux had not been some few years in the Neapolitan police without having taught himself the scientific use of the dagger. He dexterously caught his companion's wrist as he dashed in, only to find his own similarly pinioned before he could strike. Then it became a question of strength and endurance as to which should first free his dagger-hand. His comrades now took heart of grace and hurried to his assistance, but, ere they could interfere, the younger man had proved the stronger. Leroux wrenched his hand free, and buried his dagger in Patroceni's side.

"Habet!" murmured the bandit, as he sank to the ground, with a cynical smile on his lips.

Leroux stood for a moment breathless and triumphant, but bleeding, for, firmly as he had struggled to hold Patroceni's wrist, he had not escaped some flesh wounds.

"Quick!" he cried, looking down upon

the prostrate foe, " carry him to the nearest
tent, and run down to the brook for the
doctor, one of you. It was a near thing for
you, signor," he continued, turning to Glanfield. " I arrived too late, I fear, to save
your comrades," and as he spoke he walked
towards Hammerton.

Mechanically, Glanfield followed him. It
needed no expert to see that Hammerton's
course was run ; he would never " stock
cards " again. But there were others to
look to besides the dead man. No less than
three of Leroux's immediate followers were
stretched upon the grass, and one of these
would never carry carbine more. By this
time the doctor had come to Wheldrake,
whom Glanfield had already picked up, and
was holding in his arms. Cyril lay with his
head upon his friend's shoulder, quite insensible. The doctor drew back the lids,
and peered into his eyes ; then rapidly tore
open his shooting-jacket and waistcoat. A
small wound, from which the blood was

slowly welling, was distinctly visible. The
doctor placed his hand on his pulse, and
then said :—

" I can't say for certain till we probe the
wound, but I should fancy no vital organ is
touched, and that this is by no means a
hopeless case. Force some spirits between
his teeth if you have any here, and he will
soon come to himself at all events. Carry
him into the tent at once, and now let us
have a look at this one," continued the
doctor, as he turned to where Sarini lay
tightly bound hand and foot.

" I don't think you need trouble much
about him," replied Jim. " There's nothing
the matter really, and he'll be quite himself
in a quarter-of-an-hour. The beggar tried
to shoot me first and knife me afterwards.
But when it came to close quarters I proved
the stronger, and was able to reciprocate
his polite attention by nearly choking the
life out of him."

Leroux had to translate this for the

benefit of the Italian medico, and he had
also had to translate that worthy's favour-
able verdict regarding Wheldrake.

At this juncture Sir Jasper arrived on
the scene. He, like the ladies, had been
aroused by the report of firearms. It must
not be supposed that the baronet had lost
much time in arriving at the spot. He
was sound asleep and in bed when the
crack of Patroceni's revolver announced
the commencement of the action, and it
must be borne in mind that the whole affair
was a matter of a very few minutes. He
had left Maude and Mrs. Fullerton in tears
of the direst dismay, fully convinced that
the butchery of their respective lovers was
in progress. Nothing but the most peremptory orders on the part of Sir Jasper had
prevented their rushing out on to the
plateau to see what was taking place. But
the baronet was very resolute on this point
and they feared to disobey. By the time
Sir Jasper had tumbled into his clothes,

partially pacified his sister and daughter, and stepped on to the plateau, the skirmish was over. That there had been sharp fighting he saw at a glance, and made his way rapidly towards where the little group were gathered round Sarini.

"Does anybody know who this fellow is?" inquired the police-agent. "He should be a man of mark amongst them. Dressed like a peasant though he is, it is easy to see he is not of their class. Besides, there is one distinct peculiarity about him."

"And what is that, Signor Leroux?" inquired the doctor, inquisitively.

"Like his chief, you see," rejoined the police-agent, "he abstained from the wine. Not that for one moment I suppose he don't drink it; but the officers never frequent the same taverns as their men."

Sir Jasper had arrived in time to hear this last remark; but it being couched in Italian he was unable to understand it. Taking off his hat to Leroux he said:

" I suppose, sir, the camp is in the hands of the police, and that I have the honour of speaking to the chief of the party who has rescued us ? "

" Signor Leroux, at your service," replied the police-agent, recognising at a glance that he was speaking to Sir Jasper Eversley. " Yes, the camp, Patroceni, and all his men, are in our hands, and you will be all at liberty to depart for Naples in two or three hours—in short, just as soon as preparations can be made for that purpose. But it has not been altogether without some loss of life. Messrs. Hammerton and Wheldrake are, I am afraid, past all our helping."

" Hammerton ? " exclaimed the baronet. " Good Heavens, how did he come here ? "

" That, Sir Jasper, I have no more idea than you have. About a quarter-of-an-hour ago I thought he was safe in Naples. Now he lies there," and he pointed to the prostrate form, over which some one had already reverently thrown a cloak.

"The game is up, I suppose," said Sarini, struggling as well as his bound hands would permit him into a sitting posture. "That cursed Englishman! His hands were like a vice. They choked the very life out of me. Feel for my poignard I could not. I wanted both my hands to try and release my throat from his deadly grip. His Excellency escaped?"

"No; he is a prisoner, and badly wounded," replied Leroux.

"Are you the leader of the police?" inquired the bandit. Leroux nodded his head in the affirmative.

"It is a marvel that you are alive," said Sarini; "if it had not been for the coward's trick you played us with the wine you would have found your task none so easy." And the bandit dropped backwards on the grass, and subsided into sullen silence.

But the feverish curiosity of the two
ladies was no longer to be suppressed. As
she made a hasty toilette Mrs. Fullerton
announced that she must know what was
going on even if she died for it.

"I declare, my hand shakes so, Maude, I
cannot fasten my dress. All that firing and
shouting must have meant an attack on the
camp; and," she continued, dropping her
voice, "something dreadful has probably
happened."

"You don't think Cyril or Mr. Glanfield
have been killed, do you?" said Maude, in
a hoarse whisper.

"I daren't think," rejoined her aunt, as
she clutched her by the wrist. "Come, we
must know," and, as she spoke, Mrs. Fullerton opened the hut-door.

Leroux's quick eye was the first to catch
sight of them.

"I think, signors," said he, hurriedly,
"one of you had better interfere. This is
hardly a fit scene for ladies. Besides, one

of your party is lying dead and another badly wounded, and women are apt to get hysterical and slightly unmanageable at such sights. My own appearance, too," he remarked, glancing down at his blood-stained clothes, " is hardly reassuring."

"He is quite right, Sir Jasper," said Glanfield. "Come along, we had better speak to them at once. Not a word about Hammerton at present, remember. They suppose him safe in Naples, and will therefore feel no anxiety about him."

But no sooner did they near the hut than Maude sprang forward.

" Cyril, where is Cyril ? " she exclaimed. " He is killed; I can see it in your faces."

" No, my dear Maude. I assure you he is not," replied Sir Jasper. "Wounded, but ——"

" You are not telling me the truth," interrupted Maude.

" He is nothing of the kind," interposed Glanfield, roughly; " he is wounded, but not seriously. The doctor says he'll come round all right. This will never do," he continued, as the girl showed symptoms of becoming hysterical. " We want you as soon as you have pulled yourselves together to take the nursing in hand, between you. Take her into the hut, Clara; and remember, we really want you, as soon as you've steadied your nerves a bit."

" It's quite true what he tells you," observed the baronet. " There has been some wild work, but we are free. And Wheldrake, though wounded, is not dangerously so. You shall know all about it as soon as you have composed yourselves."

" It's very odd," said Glanfield, as he and Sir Jasper walked back towards the tent. " I can't make out how Hammerton came here; and, now I think of it, what has become of Jackson ? "

The police-agent here met them. " I've just been talking to the doctor," he said. " He thinks, with care, there is no reason why Signor Wheldrake should not do well. But, for Patroceni, my dagger bit too deep. It was a life-and-death struggle, signors. One cannot be delicate with one's blows upon such an occasion. If I had not killed him he would have killed me."

Suddenly a couple of the gendarmes were seen coming towards them from the edge of the wood, with a prisoner between them. The portly butler looked perfectly dazed. His rubicund face had lost its colour, and his legs shook under him.

" We found this man," explained one of the escort, " hiding in the wood. We presume he belongs to the English milord's party."

" Well, Jackson," exclaimed Glanfield, as the butler approached them, "you seem to have been having a lively night of it. What is the matter with you?"

"It's no use, Mr. Glanfield, I can't stand it. I'm not steeped in crime yet. I can't look on at murder and keep on anticipating

my latter end. I'd sooner it came at once
and was all over than go on in this way. I
suppose they are going to settle us all now.
Such a night as I've had! Do you know,
sir"—and he dropped his voice to a mysterious whisper—" that the wood is full of
murdered men? That Count and his lieutenant are insatiable monsters. They must
have been murdering the whole blessed
night."

" What! did you see them?"

" No, Mr. Glanfield, I only saw them
commit one—there was only one left alive
when I got to the scene of carnage. He
was a trying to wake the other corpses.
When that Count and Sarini came upon
him he grovelled for his life. Of course,
I don't know what he said, but I saw the
poor creature grovel; and then that Count,
he shot him just as you might a rabbit,
Mr. Glanfield; and then I crept away and
hid myself in the wood, and there I've
been shivering and shaking ever since, till

these two policemen found me and dragged
me out, that is, if they are policemen.
The Count and his head-man were dressed
like peasants this morning. I shall die of
horror if I am not taken out of this
charnel-house; and as for Count Patroceni,
whether he shoots me or not I don't
care."

"Well, your troubles are at an end, Jackson," said Sir Jasper. "The police have
had the best of it. We are free men and
shall commence our return journey to
Naples this afternoon."

"And these murderers," said Jackson,
glancing around him with scared looks,
"are they still at large? If that Count
is loose we shall never have a quiet night's
rest until we get back to England."

"You may set your mind at ease," remarked Glanfield. "Count Patroceni's hours
are sped, and as for his band they are to
a man in the hands of the police."

"He didn't leave many to fall into the

hands of the police," rejoined Jackson. "They're all lying dead by the side of the brook there."

Then the doctor emerged from the tent.

"He is going fast," he said quietly. "You struck home, Signor Leroux—an internal hemorrhage has set in. He is very anxious to know how the Signor Wheldrake is, and he is also very desirous of seeing you, signor," continued the doctor, addressing Glanfield. "Perhaps you would not mind coming to him at once, for he is sinking so rapidly that I cannot undertake to say how long he will be conscious or capable of speech."

Glanfield followed the doctor into the tent, where the dying man lay stretched on his pallet-bed. His naturally sallow complexion was somewhat blanched, but his dark eyes still glittered with all the fierce, untameable light of yore.

"Ah, Mr. Glanfield," he said, "I am glad to have the opportunity of saying good-bye to you. A fine moral lesson this, to a lover of the racecourse like you. Never despair: luck may always turn at the last moment. I bear you no malice, though by this time, if the police had not intervened, I should have shot you ruthlessly under the necessities of the situation. I have become a brigand by force of circumstances; and you know that our profession would very speedily become almost useless if we did not impress these two facts upon the public:— first, that treachery to us means death; secondly, that if our prisoners fail to redeem their lives we take them. Well, it was a close shave, but the cards ran all your way at the finish, and you have won the trick. I am not one to whimper because I have lost the game; and there is one comfort," he continued, with a cynical smile, "they will not be able to enforce the penalties for the revoke. My time has come. I am glad to hear that Mr. Wheldrake is likely to do well. I am getting faint. Give me a strong dose of that spirits and water on the table there; it will give me strength for a little longer."

He swallowed two or three mouthfuls from the cup that Glanfield silently handed him.

" That's better," he muttered. " He, like you," he continued, " is a victim to the exigences. Tell him the baccarat here is played as we played it at Wrottsley. Robert Coleman, the footman — Robert Coleman, don't forget the name—he was Hammerton's confederate ; find him, and he can tell you everything. And now good-bye," and the Count extended his hand.

Glanfield clasped it, and, as he said afterwards, " It was a queer sensation, shaking hands with a man who had deliberately determined on your extinction a few hours before."

" Sarini is a prisoner, I suppose ? " said the Count. " If he is not too badly hurt let them bring him here. I should like to see him again before I go."

A few minutes more and Sarini, closely guarded, entered the tent. By the police-agent's orders they had however removed his bonds, and the bandit was enabled to walk freely up to the bedside of his dying chief.

" Farewell, old comrade. I have got my death-wound at last. It was a strange device by which they trapped us; and if by any chance you escape from their toils once more give the police-agent who planned this *ruse*—I thought to have settled with him myself, but——" and he motioned to Sarini to stoop down to hear what he had to say.

Sarini bent his head to listen to the dying man's last injunctions.

" I have dealt with two of our betrayers, —Hammerton and Giovanni," whispered Patroceni. " I leave you to settle with the third. Should you escape, avenge me on that fox, Leroux."

" If ever I should regain freedom I swear it," replied Sarini, in a low whisper.

Patroceni feebly clasped his old comrade's hand for a few seconds, then murmured " good-bye," and turned away his face.

The doctor promptly ordered the tent to be cleared ; and when next he went to look at his patient the famous bandit had fallen into that sleep that knows no waking.

CONCLUSION.

LEROUX'S prognostications about their all leaving the camp in the afternoon were not destined to be realised. To begin with, although a doctor had accompanied the police force they had no ambulances on which to move the wounded men, and the doctor was peremptory on that point. He said that Wheldrake and one of the others must be conveyed to Naples with very great care. Any roughing it would inevitably bring on high fever, and in the second place the brigands recovered so slowly from the very strong narcotic that had been administered to them that the marching them into Naples was utterly impracticable. That little knot, just opposite the stepping-stones, who had drunk the deepest, and with whom the revel had been most prolonged, were as yet by no manner of means to be roused. The whole band had of course been thoroughly disarmed, and were now carefully guarded. Leroux had himself seen each thoroughly searched, and that all their knives, poignards, or pistols were secured.

The police-agent felt there was nothing for it but to send into Naples for ambulances, to order carriages to come from thence, and meet them on the Amalfi road, and simply remain where he was until the next morning.

It may easily be supposed that Maude was now all impatience to go to her lover's bedside. She protested that she was quite calm; that her place was there, and that it was cruel not to allow her to see him. Her

father and Glanfield parried these attacks as
best they might; but Mrs. Fullerton, who
had a fellow-feeling for her niece, was not
to be so easily repulsed. She got hold of
the doctor, set the whole case before him,
and at length extracted fom him an admission that if the young lady promised to
control herself, and that his patient, when
he awoke, showed no symptoms of aggra-
vated fever, he thought there would be very
little harm in her doing so.

"He is at the present time in a calm
slumber, due, chiefly, to a strong composing
draught that I have administered to him.
But, I dare say that, in some two or three
hours, he will rouse himself."

But Maude, having obtained that much
permission, at once took matters into her
own hands. She glided quietly into the
tent, and, seating herself on a box by the
bedside, sat still and motionless, watching
her lover.

It was mid-day before he showed signs of

restlessness. He tossed a bit on his couch, murmured indistinctly, and then, as he roused himself, his lips syllabled the word " water ! "

She had a cooling drink by her side, and in a moment had raised the tumbler to his parched lips. He swallowed a few mouthfuls, and then said :

" Where am I ? What does it all mean ? Maude, my dearest, you here ? Ah ! I remember now. I ran to Glanfield's assistance, but was shot down. My side is very sore, and I feel terribly weak. But how did you come here ? "

" We are never going to part again, Cyril. They have given me leave to nurse you, and I will soon have you well again, darling, when I once get you down to Naples. We are to stay here for the night, while they get ambulances, carriages, and things to carry you and the others into the city."

" What others ? Tell me what has happened."

"I will, Cyril, if you promise not to talk.
You must know that there are others hurt
besides you. The police attacked the camp,
and have captured the whole band; but
there was fighting over it, and several of
them were badly wounded—Count Patroceni
himself, I believe, mortally. The doctor
says you are all right, and will come round
with careful nursing; and I will take care,
my own, that you don't want for that; and
now, you mustn't talk any more. I have
promised not to let you excite yourself. Try
and go to sleep again."

"I'll do my best, Maude; but I can't say.
I think there is much hope of it. Is Jim
Glanfield all right?"

"Yes, Mr. Glanfield is quite unhurt. I
heard him say that he had pretty nearly
choked the life out of somebody, so I am
afraid that is more than his assailants can
say: and now not another word."

"And when did you say we were to leave
here?

But Maude shook her head, put her finger on her lips, and resumed her old seat on the box.

In the course of the afternoon Sir Jasper went to have one more look at his luckless nephew. The body had been moved from the place where he had been slain, and was now placed in the same tent with his murderer. The two men lay side by side, all rancour and hatred between them extinguished by the universal destroyer. It might be said that they had mutually cost each other their lives; for, had it not been for Patroceni's ill-starred visit to England, and all that came of it, the probabilities are Sir Jasper and his party would never have set foot in Italy. The baronet has drawn back the sheet that covers them, and is gazing mournfully into the two faces, set in all the calm placidity of death. Softened as men's faces are

> " Before decay's effacing fingers
> Have swept the lines where beauty lingers."

Yes, " the rapture of repose" was there. These two restless spirits slept as tranquilly as if their lives had been less turbulent.

" They are both gone, Sir Jasper," said Glanfield, in a low tone; " it's not a twelve-month since they blackened poor Cyril's name at Wrottsley, and they have both expiated the crime. I'm not much of a moralist, but it looks as if Providence checked such sins as theirs off rather rapidly. Well! the Count cleared Cyril's name before he died.

" Do you mean to say," said the baronet, in a whisper, as he quietly replaced the sheet, " that Wheldrake can be proved innocent ? "

" Yes; it is no place to speak of it here. I don't want to pass harsh judgment over those gone to their account and yet lying unburied; but I can explain everything that took place that night at Wrottsley, and as soon as we get to England pledge myself to produce their confederate."

"Only do that, Glanfield, and you will make me the happiest man in England."

Glanfield's sole reply was a hearty hand-grip, and then the two men left the tent.

As the day wore on the brigands slowly began to recover; they had slept off their opiate and came to themselves in various states of sorrow and sadness. Recovery from a severe opiate is of itself apt to be woefully depressing; but when to that you add the awaking to find yourself in the hands of the police, with a vista of imprisonment, the galleys, or possible execution before you, the salt of existence seems indeed to have lost its savour. A more crestfallen crew than these men of the mountain it was scarcely possible to picture. Their captors treated them with contemptuous good-nature; but it is to be regretted that one denizen of the camp showed undue exultation at the discomfiture of his foes. Old Jackson could not resist walking about amongst them and giving vent to chuckles of satisfaction and sarcastic taunts at their present positions.

"You wine-swilling pigs! this is what comes of not taking your liquor like gentlemen! It's time savages like you were suppressed! Savages who don't know what's due to upper-servants! The idea of leaving a man in my position to sleep out on the grass all night as if he were a hare! You will see what nice little lodgings they will find for you when they get you into Naples." In short, old Jackson's conduct was far from magnanimous when he found himself on the winning side.

In the course of the next day Leroux found himself ready to move. Wheldrake had passed a good night, and the doctor's other cases were progressing favourably. The brigands were handcuffed two and two. Sarini was escorted with a special guard, and the *cortège* moved down the mountain by the nearest cut to the Amalfi road, where carriages were waiting to convey Sir Jasper and his party back to Naples.

Their arrival created no little curiosity in the city. People flocked to get a glimpse of the famous bandit, little dreaming that his remains and those of Captain Hammerton were in the covered litter that followed the *cortège*—indeed, as the police with their prisoners passed through the street, Sarini was generally mistaken for his dead chief. As soon as they were comfortably installed in their hotel, the death of Hammerton was broken to Mrs. Fullerton and Maude, and the two women were unfeignedly shocked at the tidings; for, whatever his sin against Maude and Wheldrake, it had been severely expiated; and how loyally he had performed his task as envoy to arrange for the ransom Leroux was able to testify.

The next day they laid him to rest in the cemetery; and even Glanfield, who judged his conduct past all extenuation, muttered a

prayer for the dead man's soul as he stood
by his grave.

It was a week or two, yet, before they
could set sail for England. Wheldrake's
return to convalescence was tedious. Although he progressed, on the whole, favourably, he was not without what are almost
inevitable in a recovery from severe illness
—"his bad days." The fever, consequent
upon his wound, clung to him, and made
Maude, at times, excessively anxious. As
for the luckless bandits, if the authorities
had been slow to take measures against
them they lost no time in meting out
punishment for their misdeeds. Sarini and
two more made a bitter ending of it one
morning at daybreak, while the remainder
were translated to the galleys for a term
of years that left small chance of their ever
again resuming their profession. Wheldrake was at last pronounced sufficiently
well to be moved, and the whole party

embarked for England without further delay. ·

On their arrival, Glanfield ordered Chisel to lose no time in discovering the whereabouts of Robert Coleman. That he had left Wrottsley they, of course, knew from Jackson; still Chisel expected to have no difficulty about laying his hand upon him. But in this they were at first doomed to disappointment. Chisel could learn no tidings of him whatever. He had come to London and, apparently, disappeared in the whirlpool of the metropolis. Glanfield, to begin with, contented himself with putting an advertisement in the papers to the effect that if Robert Coleman would call upon Messrs. Seeling and Whax (his solicitors) he would hear of something to his advantage. But some days passed and this elicited no response. Mr. Coleman, it may be remembered, was in the strict retirement of one of her Majesty's gaols, and, consequently, not likely to see the journals.

Glanfield was talking this over in the smoking-room of this club one evening with an intimate friend of both his and Wheldrake's, and explaining to him why he was so anxious to find this Robert Coleman.

"What to clear Cyril Wheldrake of a false imputation of card-sharping? By Jove! you know, the man must be found. Just let me look at the advertisement. In all the dailies, you say?" and as he spoke Glanfield's companion rose and fetched a paper from an adjoining table. "Oh," he continued, "here it is, 'something to his advantage. Apply to Seeling and Whax, Lincoln's Inn Fields.' That is not quite the sort of advertisement, my dear Jim, to fetch him. I know the sort of firm, old family solicitors, very guarded and cautious. No, no, this won't do; advertise to-morrow: 'Twenty pounds reward to any-one who will give information concerning the whereabouts of Robert Coleman. Apply to James Glanfield, Esq. Blenheim Club, Pall Mall.'

You'll find that you'll get an answer to that before the week's out."

Glanfield followed his friend's advice, and speedily found his prediction realised.

Mr. Samuel Bludd has only flitted across these pages in fugitive fashion—has indeed no bearing on this history, except for his fleeting connection with Robert Coleman. It may remembered, after squeezing that unfortunate till he had left him as dry as a sucked orange, he adopted him as a companion in fraud; that the result was disastrous; and that the penalty was paid, as is too often the case, by the neophyte, while the hardened criminal went scatheless. To a man of Mr. Bludd's pursuits the perusal of what is termed the "Agony Column" in the daily papers was a mere matter of business. He never expected to hear of anything to his advantage, but he had over and over again found advertisements that with a little dexterity on his part he had made turn out highly profitable to himself. No sooner did he catch sight of this notice than Mr. Bludd thought to himself, '" I can furnish them with the necessary information. This don't look like a plant, and to pick up a twenty-pound note is worth running a little risk for; I'll chance it." Accordingly Glanfield received a line from him the next day to say that the writer, for the consideration advertised, would put him in possession of the information he required, provided no further questions were asked, and would call upon him at the Blenheim about six o'clock that afternoon.

True to his tryst Mr. Bludd arrived at that hour, and was immediately shown into a small room off the hall devoted by the members to seeing people on business.

Glanfield was not the man to make a muddle of an interview of this nature. He reckoned up Mr. Bludd at a glance, and knew exactly the line to take with a man of his calibre.

" Now, Mr. Bludd," he said, as he entered

CONCLUSION. **265**

the room where that gentleman was awaiting him, "let's understand each other at
once; there's nothing like plain speaking
on these occasions. 'No further questions
asked,' I presume means that you and
Robert Coleman have been engaged in
some affair in which publicity is not de-
sirable. I want to know nothing about
that. I mean no harm to Robert Coleman;
on the contrary, there is another twenty
pounds for him if he will only answer
two or three questions I wish to put to
him—questions which can by no possibility
bring him into any trouble."

A very shrewd man was Mr. Bludd, and
he had already divined that Robert Coleman was wanted with reference to the
Wrottsley card case. But then the papers
had rung with the Amalfi tragedy. Mr.
Bludd knew perfectly well that Hammerton
was dead, and that when his "tear friend,"
Robert Coleman, was released from prison
the game of *chantage* was over.

VOL. III.   T

"Very well, sir," he replied. "I knows a gentleman when I sees him, bless you. Write me a cheque for the twenty pounds, and I will give you Robert Coleman's address."

"You're a little too fast, my friend," replied Glanfield, curtly. "I must have a little more guarantee as to the truth of your story."

"Look here, Misther Glanfield, write me a cheque dated the day after to-morrow. That will give you to-morrow to see if it is right or not. Go to Millbank and ask for Robert Coleman under the name of Charles Harrison. That's right, s'help me. He's in there doing time."

"That'll do," said Jim, and sitting down to the table he wrote a cheque for the amount and handed it over to Mr. Bludd. "Then," he said, "if I find your information all right you'll get your money; if not, you'll find that cheque stopped at the bank."

" That'll do, Mr. Glanfield. That's right, sir. You'll find Robert Coleman to-morrow. Good-night, sir. I only wish there was somebody else's address you were wanting at the same price. Dash me!" muttered the Jew, as he walked down the club steps, " how I should like to sell the whole London Directory on the same terms!"

Glanfield went down to Millbank the next day, armed with an order to see Robert Coleman, alias Charles Harrison. He found the ex-footman in a very crest-fallen condition, and only too glad on hearing of Hammerton's death, and the promise of a twenty-pound note on his dis-charge, to confess his share of the Wrottsley business. He was, he said, paid by Ham-merton to wait until the card-table broke up, and, when the players retired to rest, he stole into the drawing-room and abstracted all the superfluous nines. " On the occa-sion of Jackson's discovery he had been so tired the previous evening that he had gone to bed, intending to get up early and re-arrange the cards; but he had overslept himself, and, when he rushed down stairs to the drawing-room, Jackson had anticipated both him and the other footman, and was already re-sorting the cards."

With Coleman's confession, written out and attested, Sir Jasper was only too glad to withdraw the remnants of his opposition to Wheldrake's marriage with his daughter; while, when Glanfield told the whole story of Patroceni's confession, supported by the written testimony of the ex-footman, club-land gladly welcomed back one of its most popular denizens within its various walls.

My story is told.   That the bells were ringing at Wrottsley, and the famous Wrottsley ale a-humming in honour of a double wedding before three months were over, must be a fact patent to all readers of this narrative; and that Jackson should regale the housekeeper's room with won-drous accounts of his adventures among the brigands may be easily conceived. In the course of years the wondrous tale so grew in the telling, that the graphic account of how he (Jackson) slew Patroceni and saved the lives of his master and his friends became quite the accepted version; and there was an undefined feeling that the Victoria Cross was by no means bestowed impartially.

THE END.

Westminster: Printed by Nichols and Sons, 25, Parliament Street, S.W.